Praise for *Sonja & Carl* by Suzanne I

"A moving tale of love, family, sacrifice, and the devastating consequences of our actions."
—*In the Hills Magazine*

"Hillier, a retired teacher and former lawyer, has created a uniquely Canadian story that tackles ambition, love, loss, and the sweetness of ordinary lives."
—Emily Reilly, *The Hamilton Spectator*

"Adult appeal although a YA novel. Strong, well-drawn characters growing in life through a plot that is entertaining and inspirational."
—Jim Misko, author of *The Path of the Wind*

"*Sonja & Carl*, the first fiction novel from Newfoundland's Suzanne Hillier, captures the nuances of Canadian culture among young adults at the turn of the 20th century."
—Mariah Wilson, *The Gauntlet*

"[Sonja's] canny observations and mordant wit propel her into the heart of things . . . Her voice is spot-on and for the reader, a chance to become immersed in an unusual page-turner."
—Norman Gorin, formerly of *60 Minutes*

"I don't usually read YA fiction . . . but the piecing together of their connection was sweet and intriguing, and quickly tragic . . . I look forward to reading [Hillier's] future works."
—Janice Carkner, Girly Book Club

"Bears similarities to Lucy Maud Montgomery's classic, *Anne of Green Gables*, though it's set at the turn of this millennium . . . the plot charges ahead like a Hollywood romantic comedy with entertaining characters that readers can easily root for."
—*Winnipeg Review*

my
best
friend
was
ANGELA BENNETT

We gratefully acknowledge the support of the Canada Council for the Arts and the Ontario Arts Council for our publishing program. We also acknowledge the financial support of the Government of Canada.

My Best Friend Was Angela Bennett is a work of fiction. All the characters and situations portrayed in this book are fictitious, unless otherwise stated. Any resemblance to persons living or dead is purely coincidental.

Cover design: Val Fullard

Library and Archives Canada Cataloguing in Publication

Title: My best friend was Angela Bennett : a novel / Suzanne Hillier.
Names: Hillier, Suzanne (Young adult writer), author.
Series: Inanna poetry & fiction series.
Description: Series statement: Inanna poetry & fiction series
Identifiers: Canadiana (print) 20210162686 | Canadiana (ebook) 20210162694 | ISBN 9781771338639
   (softcover) | ISBN 9781771338646 (EPUB) | ISBN 9781771338653 (PDF)
Classification: LCC PS8615.I422 M92 2021 | DDC C813/.6—dc23

Printed and Bound in Canada.

Published in Canada by
Inanna Publications and Education Inc.
210 Founders College, York University
4700 Keele Street, Toronto, Ontario M3J 1P3
Telephone: (416) 736-5356 Fax (416) 736-5765
Email: inanna.publications@inanna.ca Website: www.inanna.ca

my
best
friend
was
ANGELA BENNETT

a novel

Suzanne Hillier

inanna poetry & fiction series

INANNA PUBLICATIONS AND EDUCATION INC.
TORONTO, CANADA

In memory of Pop

1. When Angie Met Danny

I REMEMBER THE SUMMER my best friend Angela met Daniel. It was the summer of 1942, just before the final year of high school in St. John's.

Summers in Newfoundland are short and not hot. When, after ten months of snow, freezing winds, and rain, the sun finally peeps out from behind the clouds, people are so relieved they head outside and take their clothes off.

It was the third week of July and said to be "boiling," although it was probably only around seventy in the sun. Angie lived next door, in a large wooden bungalow similar to ours. We met by our cedar hedge, hugged, and walked toward the bus stop. I saw Edgar Clarke standing still and watching us—or most likely Angie—from across the street. We waited together, laughing as usual, then got on a bus and headed for Bowring Park, about four miles west of home.

To the left of the park's entrance was a small pond with a few wooden rowboats facing a tall copper statue of Peter Pan looking down at us, blowing on a flute. To the right was a proud caribou on a mound of earth. If you continued on the gravel road you would reach The Bungalow, where they sold hot dogs and warm potato chips sprinkled with salt and vinegar. There were tennis courts and a large, brown, rectangular swimming pool, always cold, with a dirt bottom and a diving board. The entire park was covered by thick clumps of maples and pines, interspersed with small and large lawns. We decided we would go for a swim, lie in the sun, and later head to The Bungalow for chips and ice cream.

"Edgar Clarke keeps staring at me." Angie sighed. "He almost cut off his foot with his lawnmower when he saw me come out of the house. He gives me the creeps."

Tall, dark, bulky Edgar lived in a two-storey bungalow across the street from the Bennetts' place. He had dropped out of Prince of Wales College the year before in order to assist his ailing father in his printing business.

"That's because you look like Betty Grable in your bathing suit," I teased.

"He's never seen me in my bathing suit and never will," Angie snapped.

Angie used to be shy, but she had started to think more of herself since being asked to sing in the school auditorium after prayers. Hettie Bennett had started Angie at piano at eight, but when it became obvious she was no virtuoso, her mother switched to singing lessons. Angie had a high flute-like soprano voice and sang with great earnestness the patriotic songs of the day, her head cocked to one side and her hands clasped in front of her.

"There'll Always Be an England" and "There'll Be Bluebirds Over the White Cliffs of Dover" were her favourites. She wanted to sing "We'll Meet Again," but was informed by our principal it was "too advanced" for the student body. Angie's singing always got thunderous applause, the boys stamping their feet to show their appreciation. She would tell me later she found all the attention embarrassing, but I suspected she loved it. She would trip from the platform flushed with pride.

"I guess Edgar wants to say he knew you when, after you start your movie career as the Newfoundland Deanna Durbin."

"Oh, shut up, Dot," she said, laughing.

We nudged each other, both giggling, and linked arms with the closeness that came from walking back and forth from school together for as long as I could remember. She knew she was getting a little high on herself with all the compliments about her voice and looks.

We pretended to be nervy and to know all about what it meant to have a woman's body. We pretended to understand what men were thinking, but we knew almost nothing. We didn't even know what oral sex was. We were sixteen and seventeen, and all we knew was that if you had sex with someone, you married him. If you didn't, you were a "bit of a girl," "a proper whore," or "a hard case." There was no pill and very few options. And if you weren't married or engaged by the time you were twenty, you were considered an old maid. This is how it worked for me and Angie, middle class and Protestant. This is what our mothers made us believe.

Angie's experience with men was limited to smiling at the servicemen who visited Bennett's Furs while she was filling in for her mother, Hettie; receiving the most valentines at Prince of Wales; and seeing musical comedies at the Capitol and Paramount Theatres, the town's two better movie houses. These movies always ended in a chaste kiss and happiness ever after. We both believed in these stories in some sense, Angie perhaps more than I did.

We got off the bus at the park's entrance. After we got off, I saw our reflections in the bus door. Dorothy Butler, too tall and too thin and too flat-chested, her straight dark hair clipped back in a roll high up from her forehead with the rest hanging lankly behind. Angela Bennett, tossing the thick curly chestnut mane that fell to her shoulders, her breasts swelling under her white blouse, her Bermuda shorts exposing milky, shapely legs.

"Bet the water will be freezing," she said. "I got a new bathing suit, a blue two-piece, really darling, with a little skirt. Mom gave me some money for filling in at the store."

"Great," I replied. "And I'll look really darling in my black Olympic one-piece."

Angie giggled and took my hand.

"Dot, in a few years you'll be glad you're so slim, when the rest of us are waddling around fat as ducks. You'll never be fat. And none of the great models have breasts."

I put an arm around her, gave her a squeeze, and forgave her for being one hundred times better-looking than I was or ever would be.

We changed, shivering in one of the wooden cubicles next to the pool, as out of the sun it was no longer warm. Angie's swimsuit showed her pale, molded figure to perfection. I tucked my hair into an ugly rubber bathing cap while Angie anchored hers with bobby pins into a curly nest on top of her head. We walked toward the pool, cold, dappled mud-grey, and uninviting.

A boy was standing by the diving board. He may have been eighteen, but he seemed somewhat older, more easy in his skin. That skin was fish-belly white, his black hair tousled, his arms muscled. He was smiling—a crooked, tough smile like Jimmy Cagney's just before he took on the gang at the end of *Public Enemy*, or like Gene Kelly's just before he started to dance.

I saw him look at Angie, and his eyes gulped her down. I looked at Angie, and she was looking back at the boy, transfixed. And I thought ... oh shit.

He ran to the end of the diving board and did a perfect dive. When he surfaced he sought her out. She kept watching but didn't smile back.

"I wouldn't want to interrupt anything," I said, "but are we going to swim?"

"You dive. I don't want to get my hair wet."

I dove, a good dive. But no one was watching. When I surfaced I saw Angie, with not a hair of her nest of curls out of place, doing a slow breast stroke across the pool. The black-haired boy was following her, swimming in circles around her underwater, breaking the surface every two minutes.

Underneath the water he can watch her legs, moving like a little pale green frog's in the muddy water.

I did the crawl right up to her, knowing she was quite capable of doing the crawl as well as I was, if not the fancy dive.

"We may as well go and get some sun," I suggested. "You must be exhausted from all your strenuous swimming." I turned and gave a hard look to the boy who was still watching.

She gave me a brief smile and an eye roll.

"Let's go," I said again. I didn't trust this boy, and I felt left out.

Behind the wooden changerooms there was a grassy incline and a lawn surrounded by pine and spruce trees, where people went to sun. The lawn was peppered with bleached bodies, and everyone was smoking because Humphrey Bogart did.

We settled ourselves on the lawn. Angie had released her curly knob, which she was now combing out carefully, and her hair bounced from her creamy shoulders. She seemed to be showing more cleavage.

"Did your new suit shrink?"

"Oh Dot, you're as bad as Mom."

Then he was standing there, the interloper, looking down at us but really looking down at Angie. "Is this spot taken?"

"I didn't buy tickets," said Angie.

Not like Angie to be a saucebox, but she was smiling, and the next thing I knew she had changed her position on the large towel she had been lying on, and he was stretched out on the towel beside her.

He shook two cigarettes from a Lucky Strikes package, placed them both between his lips, lit up, and moved one between Angie's lips. Bette Davis and Paul Henreid in *Now, Voyager* came to mind, and I guessed he'd seen the preview of the movie. I was struck dumb by his blatant familiarity. It was sexier than making love, I was sure, having had no experience with either smoking or lovemaking.

Angie took a deep drag, turned ashen, and started hacking. We all laughed, even Angie.

"Angie doesn't smoke," I explained, and then added accusingly, "You made her sick."

He inhaled deeply, as if to make up for her obvious inexperience, and stretched out his hand, touching her ivory shoulder, a gentle touch.

"Sorry, Angie. I'll be better to you from now on."

Angie bestowed a nauseated smile on the stranger. She had obviously forgiven him, even before he'd asked. I had the uneasy feeling she'd forgive him anything.

I sat on the grass, my arms tight around my bony knees, watching them as they lay in the sun together. I looked at their bodies, white as marble, taking in the warmth, so aware of each other, yet not touching.

"You are?" he asked, after a few minutes.

"Angela Bennett, but my friends call me Angie, and this is Dorothy Butler."

"Pleased to meet you," he said without looking in my direction. "Danny Flaherty, Daniel really, but no one calls me that."

Later we went to The Bungalow for chips. The lawn in front was full of servicemen, all lying on the grass eating chips with local girls. Danny insisted on paying, and we all headed for the bus to go back to the West End. He took one of the two-seater bus benches, and patted the other side for Angie to join him. "Do you mind, Dottie?" she asked.

"Why would I mind?" I answered, furious.

I heard drifts of their conversation. He had been attending Holy Cross but was not returning for the final year. He was working part time and hoped for full time come September. He lived in one of the railway houses, just up the Avenue.

"Good that we're so close," he remarked cheerfully to Angie as we got off the bus. Then, before we started to head in different directions, he continued, "'cept you probably got your own room, an' yer ol' man's second home's not the Star of the Sea Tavern."

The thought of Angie's father, senior partner of an accounting firm, frequenting a tavern—indeed even thinking of such a thing, with Hettie monitoring his every word, if not thought—amused me, and I gave an inappropriate hoot. Danny looked at me, raising a sharp black eyebrow over an eye as blue as the blueberries growing on the Brigus Barrens, while Angie tossed me a rare scowl.

"Oh well," he shrugged. "At least we're employed Micks."

He brushed a kiss against Angie's cheek that burned a bright pink.

"I'll see you, you know that."

He sauntered up the street, cocky as could be, pausing only to light one of his Lucky Strikes, not even looking back, his black leather bomber jacket as shiny as his hair in the dying light of a cooling July afternoon.

"That was rude," said Angie.

"Rude," I replied. "You think I'm rude? He's so cheeky I can't believe it! Moving in on you like that and kissing you goodbye. Your mother would die. And taking for granted you'll see him again. I don't even believe he works."

"He plays cards."

"How do you know that? You mean he gambles? Gambling isn't a job."

"He plays poker with some rich kids and some of the enlisted men. He told me that on the bus. He does well. They call him Lucky Danny."

"Probably cheats them blind." Then, using Ma's expression, I said, "Nerve like a toothache."

"Never thought you were such a snob, Dot."

I started to defend myself, but stopped. Angie was my best friend, and I wasn't going to lose her because of some slick young low-life. If she ever needed my friendship it was now. I had to protect her.

"Sorry, ducky, my mouth's too big. Pop always says if I wasn't a girl, I'd be a great lawyer."

This was a time when the only woman I knew who worked outside the home was Hettie Bennett. There were schoolteachers, nurses, and Pop's secretaries, but they didn't count.

"It's okay, Dottie. Maybe I'm being too sensitive."

She linked up my arm with hers, smiled, and forgave me.

Their relationship didn't end there. I knew it wouldn't. I'd known it the moment I saw them lying together on Angie's towel, carved in marble in the sun in Bowring Park, and when he brushed her shoulder with his hand.

I knew this was only the beginning.

2. Kitchen Conversations

IT WAS THE DAY AFTER the Bowring Park visit and Hettie Bennett, who had closed Bennett's Furs for two weeks during the month of July, was enjoying a cup of tea with Ma at the kitchen table. I watched her pale angular face and stiff grey perm as I stood slouched against the frame of the kitchen door and listened.

"It took them long enough," she sniffed. "Now they're singing 'Praise the Lord and Pass the Ammunition' as if they're the saviours of the world, all while poor London was being blitzed to death and they did nothing."

Ma nodded. "Terrible," she agreed.

We were Britain's oldest colony, and we fought for the King. And we were Protestant, which led Hettie to her next favourite topic: "And what does His Nibs think of what's happening to this Avenue?"

"He never discusses it. I think some of them are clients."

"You'd think," said Hettie, picking up one of Ma's still-warm date crumbles, and taking a sharp bite with her long, bright false teeth, "as a lawyer he'd show more concern for our real estate prices. We'll have a slum at the end of our street, and they'll be filling their bathtubs with coal like they've done everywhere else."

She took a deep breath and another sip of tea in order to continue. "I hear a Mrs. Biden's had twenty-one children—she's as familiar to St. Clare's as any nurse—and she can't remember their names, although I guarantee they never miss Mass. All they do is drink, reproduce, and brawl."

"Such big families," murmured Ma. "I worry for the children."

"Don't waste your time, Lil," snapped Hettie, draining her cup and reaching for another date crumble. "They'll be just like the parents."

At this point I left the kitchen door to return to my reading, hoping that Angie had seen the last of Danny Flaherty.

"Did your boyfriend visit today?" asked Pop, smiling. "I thought I smelled a whiff of something when I came in the front door.

Ma's "boyfriend" was Evans, who came twice a week for handouts for his large crew living in a wooden shack on the Southside Hills in the area known as The Brow. There were fewer door-knockers now, as employment had increased with the war, but Evans remained faithful—and unemployable. Ma refused to give money, fearing it would be spent on screech, but kept Evans supplied with cooking basics, and in return he'd do the occasional chore. I sat on the wooden steps leading to our upstairs and watched them.

"A cup of tea, Mr. Evans?" Ma asked, as he stood inside our front porch. I knew she kept a special cup for him which she boiled after use.

"Don't mind if I do, Missus."

"The usual sugar?" she asked, and then gave her own answer: "Three heaping teaspoons."

"Forgetting rationing?" I called out, but Ma ignored me.

"Wouldn't mind a swig of somethin' stronger—feel a chill comin' on."

"You won't find that in this house," answered Ma, a WCTU member. Then I heard her sing from the kitchen, loud enough for Evans to hear, "Softly and tenderly Jesus is calling."

Evans waited a respectful interval and then, having finished his tea, called out, "My young fella's joined the Royal Navy." I'd seen his son only once, when he'd come with Evans to attempt to resurrect Ma's failed victory garden, and my only memory was two icicles of green snot hanging from a freckled pug-nose.

Ma suddenly appeared and took Evans's cup. "Might be the making of him," she said.

"As long as he don't get torpedoed and drownded," Evans replied.

Ma said nothing more, but when I followed her into the kitchen I noticed she packed more food than usual for him, even a large piece of the special fruitcake she'd made herself.

"Hettie was here today," Ma informed Pop, as she placed a plate of fried cod, boiled potatoes, cabbage, and turnips in front of him that night.

"And?"

"On and on about the railway houses as usual."

"We're in a war, our boys are being slaughtered, and this is all the battleaxe can talk about," snorted Pop. "Too bad that poor henpecked husband of hers has nothing to say. These people are employed—doesn't she know that? When I remind them to turn off their lights during the drill, they're downright civil and obliging."

Pop took his air-raid warden duties seriously, wearing his hard helmet and white armband, and canvassing the entire street for forbidden lights as soon as the sirens started. But no planes came, and no bombs fell. The sirens went off anyway, so we sat in the darkness to practise, just in case, waiting for the all-clear and listening to Winston Churchill on the radio, our spirits soaring from just the sound of his voice. Then, when he and Roosevelt met on board a ship anchored in Placentia Bay, we knew we were really on the map, and not just a rocky island full of cod and tuberculosis that Britain sent its drunken aristocrats to govern.

Every day the papers carried notices of missing servicemen, all presumed dead.

"Gertie Russell's boy is missing—her only son," said Ma sadly. "A fine, decent boy."

"Terrible," said Pop, and he stopped eating. When he started again, he turned to me, obviously a more pleasant distraction. "Eat up, Dottie—you'll need your strength for next year. I'm expecting another report card as good as your last one. University's coming."

University was not taken seriously for most girls, who were thought to be merely shopping for husbands, but Pop was different. He was interested in my grades, Ma less so. He'd wanted a boy, she'd confided to me once, and, she complained, treated me like one. At least he'd made the best of my arrival.

I'd have to concentrate on my studies; there were no other choices. Then I thought of Angie.

3. The Enabler

"I WANT TO SEE *Casablanca*," Angie said.

"We've already seen it."

"It's a little different this time," she replied. "Danny is coming."

He didn't wait long, and I knew what would happen. I would be the third wheel, leaving and arriving home with Angie, but in between would be Lucky Danny with his Lucky Strikes and lopsided grin.

"We'll sit at the back," instructed Danny. "You can sit farther up 'cause you don't want to miss the dialogue."

Danny had no doubt seen *Casablanca* before as well, and I knew he wasn't really worried about my missing the dialogue. His motive, I suspected, was to get Angie in the back row of the Paramount Theatre and neck up a storm with her.

I glanced at Angie, and she was looking at Danny, certainly not objecting to the fact that her best friend had been directed to sit alone in the theatre while she cuddled with Danny Flaherty.

Just after Rick Blaine asked Sam to play "As Time Goes By," I looked back at the occupants of the last row. They were kissing, and Danny's hand was down the neck of Angie's blouse. He was feeling her left breast. She didn't seem to mind, and she even had her arm around his neck. Anyone could see that watching Ingrid Bergman and Humphrey Bogart was the last thing on their minds.

Things were moving much too fast, and I was part of it. I tried to enjoy the movie and imagine I looked like Ingrid Bergman, who I'd read was way taller than Humphrey Bogart. But all I could think of was what Hettie Bennett's reaction would be when someone told her—and someone would tell her—that her daughter was sneaking around behind her back with an Irish tough and acting cheap in the last row of the Paramount Theatre. And that her best friend was helping it all happen.

As we waited for the bus, I noticed Angie's face was red all up one side. They were holding hands, and Danny was smiling away as if he'd just won hundreds in one of his card games.

"I want Danny to hear me sing in September."

As if on cue, Danny sang two bars of "As Time Goes By" in a glorious tenor, never once taking his eyes off Angie.

"He can sing," sang Angie. "We can do duets together."

"Why don't you both go to Hollywood?"

I left them at the bus stop and walked to the next one. The bus was late as usual, so I made it. They were sitting at the back, both looking very serious, when I sat down on the seat in front of them.

"You mad, Dot?" asked Angie.

"We wouldn't want you to think we're not grateful for all you're doin'," said Danny.

What could I say? How do you put a mixture of envy, concern, and anger into words?

"I just don't want trouble."

Angie kept on seeing him, telling her mother she was visiting me. This meant she had to come over to my house first, then slip out and meet him on Topsail Road, next to the General Protestant Cemetery. They would, she confided, walk along the paths among the tombstones, or sit on one of the two benches under a large cluster of giant pines.

The July nights were warm during the summer of 1942. Angie told me of their nights together: sitting close under swaying scented pines, with only the sound of an occasional car chugging up the unpaved Topsail Road. She said it was "so romantic." Sometimes, she told me, they'd even sing together.

But in August, everything changed. Mothers and wives received telegrams and saw notices in the daily papers. They sat looking into space and then collapsed into months of tears. There were 3,367 casualties, and 916 Canadians dead, many of them our boys, slaughtered at Dieppe.

"They killed our boys first. Sent them out first, the Brits did, as if our boys didn't matter," Ma cried.

"They made mistakes, gave the wrong orders, and our boys were finished, dying on the beaches or blown away in the sky."

No one wanted to believe it, and there was sorrow filled with anger.

There were masses at St. Patrick's and at the basilica, where the priests prayed of accepting the will of God and about everlasting life. At Gower Street United, the Reverend Tobias Noseworthy preached a two-hour sermon on not second-guessing the goodness of God and the congregation sang, "Oh, hear us when we cry to Thee, for those in peril on the sea."

But our boys were gone, and they weren't coming back.

The red streetcars clanged over the cobblestones along Water Street, full of grey-faced, tight-lipped, red-eyed women, women whose sons and husbands had disappeared.

The pages of *The Daily News* and *The Evening Telegram* carried pictures of them all, with their names and regiments underneath, smiling away at the camera, smiling at death.

Ma studied each picture, sighing at names she recognized. Then I heard her gasp. One of those killed was Brian Evans of the Royal Militia.

"And I said that'd be the making of him," she sobbed. "Wish I hadn't said that. Evans said it was the Navy, not the Royal Militia. Evans had a premonition. I wish I'd done more. I will," she told Pop and me, "prepare a good dinner for Evans the next time he comes. I'll even give him a shot of brandy if he wants it. He can sit at the kitchen table instead of standing inside the porch—doesn't matter how bad he smells."

But Evans never came again.

It was after Dieppe and just before school began that things started to become even more intense between Angie and Danny. There was not a day when they didn't succeed in being together. August 30 was Danny's eighteenth birthday, and he had managed to buy a fourth-hand Ford for taking Angie to various beaches and movie houses. On his birthday, he was taking Angie on a memory trip to Bowring Park and then out for dinner at Diana Sweets. I was invited as well in my usual role as cover. I was tired of it and hurt. I felt like I was being used, and I missed my former closeness with Angie, who I now had to share with the always-present Danny.

"Do you know what an enabler is, Angie?" I asked in my snottiest voice, just having learned the word myself.

Angie caught her lower lip between her teeth as she always did when she was thinking or upset. She hated confrontation—which was why she hadn't told Hettie about Danny.

"It's me—that's what an enabler is. Me, the way I am with you and Danny, 'cause you're too cowardly to even bring him to your house and say, 'This is my boyfriend who I've been necking around with for six weeks when I told you I was with Dot. He's Catholic, a high school dropout, and unemployed. He lives with his eight brothers and sisters in one of the railway houses, and, oh yes, his father's a drunk. But employed. And he gives me hickeys on my neck.'"

The last crack was unforgiveable. I was referring to a large red suck mark that Danny had produced on her pale little neck during one of their graveyard sessions and Angie had shown to me in a moment of confidence.

Her eyes started to fill up, and I felt guilty, but not guilty enough to stop, so I tried another tactic.

"How do you suppose it affects Danny to think you're ashamed of him, that you won't even have him inside the door? Bet you've met his family."

"Yes," she sighed, "I met his family. His mother's a little large and loud, quite pleasant though. She said I was pretty, asked if my mother owned Bennett's Furs, and asked me to have a cup of tea. The kids were a bit wild. Danny shares a bedroom with three brothers. It's a different way of life, and Mom would really turn her nose up. They're not people she'd mix with."

"Perhaps you shouldn't either."

She turned and looked at me, with those big light-green eyes of hers silver with tears, and said with wonder, "But Dottie, I really love him."

A few days later, Angie ranted, "I really hate Mom. I hate her. She hurt Danny's feelings, and he says he'll never darken our door again. I told her a friend was dropping by, and it was a big deal for him. He even borrowed a suit from one of the guys he gambles with and bought a tie. He looked really handsome. He was polite too. He shook her hand and bowed and said 'How do you do,' really formal.

"She just stood there, even wiped her hand on her skirt after he shook it. She had all her silver service out—stuff we never use—trying to look like royalty. Then she started to question him.

"He pretended he was working and that he'd finished grade eleven. She asked him how long we'd known each other, and he lied about that too.

"She said, 'You realize Angela won't be seventeen until October,' and added, 'we have great aspirations for her future.'

"Did you ever? First I'd heard of it.

"Then she asked him the size of his family, and when he said he had eight brothers and sisters, she rolled her eyes and said, 'Dear God, these people breed like maggots.'

"Danny said, 'Yeah, an' this maggot has got to go.'

"When I showed him to the door, he said, 'I can't come to your house again.'

"After he left, she turned to me and said, 'I really thought you'd do better than that, Angela.'

"I told my mother I hated her. She said she never wanted to set eyes on Danny again."

So we were back again to Angie lying and me covering for her.

In September, just after school began, we drove ten miles to Topsail Beach because Angie said she wanted to see the moon shining on the water. I was in the back seat, and Angie and Danny were in front. The sun was setting, the sky a pale orange with little brush strokes of purple. When we reached the beach, we all got out, and I sat on a rock and watched the waves lap up against the small round stones.

There was a little wooden gazebo with a jukebox just off the beach. Danny put a dime in it, and it started to play "We'll Meet Again." He and Angie danced, slow and close, just swaying together, barely moving.

I wished I had a boyfriend. I wished I could find someone tall enough for me. I wished Angie and Danny could always be together, even if it meant Angie moving into a railway house and having ten children.

Then the shadows appeared and a round silver moon came out and brushed a choppy crystal path all the way to Bell Island. We looked at it for a while, the three of us, Angie and Danny with their arms around each other, and then we went home.

There were no jobs for Danny. He tried Fort Pepperell, local construction, even the sawmill off Shaw Street. He still played cards, and landed a few "fish" or "marks," as he called them, from Fort Pepperell and the Canadian Barracks at Buckmaster's Field. But he needed a "stash" if he was going to attract high rollers. I suspected he thought of every job prospect as it would appear to Hettie Bennett. Probably nothing seemed good enough.

"I could drive hack," he admitted to us. "But what would Angie's mom think?"

"Never mind that," Angie said. "Her feelings are not important."

But of course they were, to them both.

Angie and I no longer walked home alone from school. Danny was always there, waiting to carry her books and walk with her the three miles along LeMarchant Road, over the Berry Hills, and through the sawmill.

I walked ahead, fuming and feeling left out, but I started to see how much he cared for her. He never missed a day. They kissed on the Berry Hills and they kissed in the sawmill, much to the amusement of the millworkers. I would stand aside looking at the South Side Hills, thinking of Evans and his missing son, while I attempted to ignore these brazen lovers.

And there were the nights. She would come from next door, look over our homework, and disappear out the back door, where he was waiting. There was no longer a car. Danny's Ford had made its last gasp, and the cost to fix it was way more than it was worth, so he sold it for parts for ten dollars. When the evenings became cooler, they had to find a new place to go. Angie told me it was the graveyard. "That's where we keep warm," she said.

"Hettie Bennett has her faults," scolded Ma, "but she's a friend of mine. Angie's up to no good, and you shouldn't be encouraging it."

In early October, just before her seventeenth birthday, Angie appeared at my house looking pale, haggard, and dishevelled, her hair a tangled halo surrounding her small white face. It was lucky Ma and Pop were at the Bar Convention dinner and I was alone.

"We had sex," she explained, "and I'm bleeding. I want to

soak my panties in your bathroom sink—I'll borrow a pair of yours. Cold water removes blood, right? I always thought Danny had been with other girls, but I don't think so. He was really clumsy at first. He didn't know what to do, and it hurt like mad, but once he got it in, it was wonderful. Oh Dot, you can't imagine how great it was just to have Danny moving inside me, even if it was on a grave in the cemetery."

"Have you thought about getting pregnant?"

"Don't think so. Anyway, I don't care. If I get pregnant then I'll have an excuse to get married."

"Angie, you can't be this dumb. You don't want to drop out of high school because you're pregnant. You'll ruin your life and reputation. I know you hate your mom, or think you do, but you can't do this to her."

But Angie wasn't listening.

It was November, and the snow had started. The flakes floated down, resting on the window ledges and covering the gardens on Craigmiller Avenue in a dazzling blanket by day and a swirling blizzard by night. Going outside meant having your face lashed by a relentless blast of wind mixed with icy snow. There would be no lovemaking on graves at the General Protestant Cemetery, or anywhere else. And Angie and Danny didn't dare try to register at the Newfoundland Hotel.

"My folks went to a party at Pepperell," said Angie when she arrived at my house. "Mom's showing her new line of seal skin jackets. I have to see Danny. You can watch for us."

Nice of her, giving me permission to be the lookout. It would be my job to stand guard while she and Danny got into whatever they were into, which, from what I understood, was sex without a "French safe"—our word for condom.

"You'll see the car as soon as they come, but we should have at least an hour and a half," said Angie.

I settled myself by the window to do my homework. I

was starting to doze when I saw the car move slowly up the driveway, all under a sheer veil of snow.

I ran to the kitchen. Angie was perched on the edge of the kitchen counter, her skirt pulled up, her legs around Danny's waist. He was cupping a small white buttock in each hand and plunging into her, while she, her head thrown back, let forth a series of cooing noises.

"They're home!" I yelled.

Danny reached for the trousers bunched around his ankles while Angie pulled down her skirt, her face taut with panic. As the front door opened, so did the back, and Danny, fly open, flew into the backyard.

"His bird will be frozen," I muttered. "You're a mental case, Angie. Don't ask me to do this again."

Hettie was so angry about the poor turnout for the fur demonstration that she was not her usual observant self. She turned on the kettle and instructed Clement to rub her neck as she felt a migraine coming on. Angie and I moved to the front room, back to my untouched books.

4. The Decision

IT WAS LATE NOVEMBER, and I knew something was happening between Danny and Angie. Danny was meeting Angie as he always did, but there was electricity in the freezing air. I walked ahead, along the sidewalk of LeMarchant Road, the sides of the walk piled with snow. When I turned around they had their heads together, and I could hear their voices rising and falling. Danny still wore his leather bomber jacket but with earmuffs, his black hair combed up high in front, stiff with frost. His boots were scuffed, and his trousers looked thin when they were blown against his legs by the constant wind.

He'd do anything for her. He'd freeze his butt just to carry her books.

On the last Friday of the month they invited me for dinner at the Candlelight on Harvey Road.

"My treat," said Angie.

I considered the reasons for the invitation. There was the usual lie: Angie would no doubt inform her mother that we were going to a movie, so I would be cast in my recurring role. Angie also knew that I had my driver's licence, and that I might convince Pop to let me borrow his car. This meant that I could drive his new Lincoln Zephyr with the huge fins, a sleek maroon body, and soft velour seats. It had even been equipped with snow chains to prevent skidding.

Pop handed me the keys with visible reluctance.

"Sure it's just you and Angela?" asked Ma.

Why was Hettie Bennett, a much more shrewd and aggressive individual than Ma, not more suspicious?

Angie had always been so compliant, so Hettie did not predict the personality change that Angie's love for Danny Flaherty had brought about, and although all of Prince of Wales College and half the neighbourhood knew Angie was still seeing Danny, no one had told Hettie. This was unusual, but no one really liked Hettie. Women who worked outside the home were viewed with suspicion, and Clement Bennett was considered "henpecked." As well, Hettie's high-pressure sale tactics at Bennett's Furs made her unpopular, as did her sharp tongue and regal ways. No doubt she thought Angie had broken up with Danny after his unfortunate house visit.

Looks good on her, her daughter messin' around with a railroad boy, they'd say.

"Isn't this wonderful?" gushed Angie, as she and Danny cuddled together on the velvety cushioned backseat of the Lincoln that had been heated up for the three-mile ride to the Candlelight.

"When I make money, I'll buy you one, one just like this. You'd look some good behind the wheel of a Lincoln, a nice blue one."

Fat chance, I thought. Then there was silence from the back seat. I glanced in the rear-view mirror, and there they were, wrapped around each other, kissing away as usual.

I swallowed the urge to tell them to stop necking in Pop's car. After all, I had refused to cooperate since Danny's scary exit at the end of what I always thought of as their kitchen-counter screw, so I knew they were starved for each other.

When they got out of the car outside the Candlelight I noticed Danny adjusting his pants that bulged suspiciously in the crotch area. *No respect*, I thought crossly. *Imagine getting a hard-on in the back of Pop's new Lincoln*. This was an expression Angie had heard from Danny and repeated to me.

I shot Angie a dirty look, but she was too busy beaming at Danny to notice.

We settled ourselves in a booth and ordered hot turkey sandwiches on white with gravy and French fries on the side. The restaurant was filled with servicemen on leave, a lot of navy boys, and the occasional officer from Fort Pepperrell.

"We want you to be the first to know," said Angie. "Danny and me, we've talked about it a lot, and Danny believes he's getting nowhere here."

"Nowhere fast," echoed Danny, lighting one of his cigarettes and then exhaling thin blue smoke.

"If he joins up, they'll put him through school when he gets out. They'll have lots of programs for ex-servicemen."

"I've joined up," interrupted Danny. "Enlisted in the Royal Canadian Navy, an' now maybe I'll be less of a maggot to Angie's mother—it'll be like puttin' lipstick on a cod."

I sat stupefied. *Were they forgetting Dieppe?* Danny was just three months past eighteen.

"Of course I'm takin' for granted that I'll be gettin' out." I watched him move restlessly on the wooden seat of the booth.

He did realize the danger, but I don't believe Angie did. She was not strong on reality, Angie, although I noticed her giving Danny an occasional anxious glance.

"We're engaged."

It was a tiny ring with a stone the size of a pinprick.

"Got lucky at poker and Silver's had a serviceman's special." He had read my mind.

He was uneducated, but had a certain intuitive shrewdness that placed him ahead of both of us. With half a chance, he'd be the owner of a used car business if he survived and got a leg up. But he didn't really need an education. It was already there.

"Have to go to the little girl's room," carolled Angie, getting up and waiting for me to join her. When I didn't, she trotted off, holding out her ring finger for all to see.

"I'm going to level with you," said Danny, smiling and frowning at the same time.

It crossed my mind that many of his lines came from a series of gangster B movies that were usually shown at the Nickel or Majestic, the town's worst theatres. It was not that he didn't mean the lines; it was just that they were scripted.

"I was going to join up before. I was going to tell them that I was eighteen, and they would've taken me. I knew I didn't have no future here. Then I met Angie in July, and I didn't want to leave her. She's not like you—in some ways she's a little girl. She really needs me to take care of her … if anything happens, I want you to take over and help her. I love her, I really do."

What he said fell on my heart like a hammer.

Angie returned and took the bill. "Last time you'll have to do that," said Danny. "Let's hope they pay me a few bucks to fight Hitler."

We left the Candlelight and settled ourselves in Pop's Lincoln again. I said, "I'm going to park down by the harbour. I have a headache from all the smoke in the restaurant, and I have to take a walk. Perhaps you two can find something to do while I'm gone."

There was silence, and I felt Angie's hand squeezing my shoulder, and when I turned around Danny winked.

I walked by the harbour. I could have driven up Signal Hill, but it was steep and hazardous. Back in the car, Danny was inside Angie, unprotected as usual, and she was letting loose the cooing doves trapped in her throat, and the back seat of Pop's Lincoln was being baptized with pure, undiluted, unrestrained love or lust—really a mixture of both.

There was a grey, steel, majestic warship docked near the wharves, and seamen were walking up and down the gangplank. Up on The Brow, the small shacks of Evans and his like shone dimly from the snow-covered hills with the small, stunted spruce poking through. I breathed in the harsh urine stench of the icy grey water.

I wondered hazily if Danny knew why he was risking his life. Was it to wipe out a blur of goose-stepping soldiers under a swastika that we saw before the main feature began? Or had he heard any of Churchill's speeches? Perhaps he understood more than he let on. Danny was full of surprises.

On Wednesday afternoon, standing outside the entrance of Prince of Wales College, there was Danny. His hair was cut short, his round navy cap sitting jauntily on one side of his head, his navy overcoat on his arm. He wore his tight navy jerkin with its sailor collar, a white singlet showing inside, and bell bottoms with stout black boots. He was leaving for Halifax on Saturday to be part of convoy SC-118, which would carry out escort duty on the Eastern Atlantic Seaboard.

Angie was beside herself with pride. I watched as she introduced him to everyone who came near as her fiancé and, in spite of his protests, pulled him inside the school. She introduced him to Miss Seaward, our class teacher, and Mr. Parsons, our principal, who had lost his only son at Dieppe. The older man said that yes, of course Danny could attend the morning prayers at the school auditorium on Friday morning.

Angie had arranged to sing "I'll Be Seeing You" and "We'll Meet Again" which, because of the war, were no longer considered too advanced for the student body. Angie, on stage that Friday morning, had never looked more beautiful, in a black dress with a V-neck and wearing high-heeled black pumps. The kittenish gestures were gone. She sang from the heart, hands by her sides, her voice true and high, with a soft piano accompaniment.

When she sang "We'll Meet Again," tears streamed down her cheeks. I turned and looked back at Danny, who was leaning forward with a hand cupped over his eyes. When she finished, there was dead silence before the applause began. I watched her step quickly from the stage. When I looked back again, Danny was gone. They were booked into The Newfoundland Hotel as Seaman and Mrs. Daniel Flaherty, Angie told me later.

"We stayed in bed all day and didn't even order room service until eight o'clock."

Danny was to check in to his ship at eleven o'clock. At eight, Hettie Bennett phoned and told me if I didn't disclose Angela's whereabouts she was calling the constabulary.

"There's a school social," I lied. "Angela was singing."

"You better not be lying, Dorothy," she said shrilly, before banging up the phone.

At ten o'clock she phoned again. She had checked. There was no school social.

"Get your mother on the phone."

"My daughter's not a liar. I'm sure if Dorothy knew where Angela was, she'd tell you. If she said a school social then she must have been confused. And I don't recommend calling the police—it causes all sorts of complications. We'll contact you if we hear anything."

She hung up the phone and turned to me. "Where's Angela?"

"Probably with Danny Flaherty. He's leaving tomorrow to join a convoy in Halifax."

"Oh, Dottie," sighed Ma. "Just as well you didn't tell Hettie. I wouldn't want to think of you cheapening yourself like that, but these are strange times. Poor young boy. They say the Atlantic's full of U-boats—but don't tell Angela that."

At eleven-thirty Angie arrived at our door, her face puffy.

"Your mother's hysterical—she says she's calling the police. I said you were at a school social, but she checked. She's really upset."

"I couldn't care less," she replied.

Danny and Angie sent letters back and forth addressed to and from a government address in Halifax. She showed me a page from one of Danny's. He wrote of his plans for their future, a new start for them both, and a marriage in the summer after her high school graduation. And how he missed her, longed and ached for her.

"The rest is about sex, Dottie," she apologized. "It wouldn't do to show you that."

"I don't want to see it. I already know too much about your sex life."

A few weeks before Christmas, she told me she was two weeks late and believed she was pregnant. I was more upset than she was.

"I warned you about this, you and Danny taking chances. There'll be a war over it, worse than what's going on in Europe. Your mother will send you off to some home for unwed mothers in Ontario, and she'll have the baby adopted."

She looked at me horrified, large liquid green eyes wide. "Dot, Danny'll get a leave and come back, or I'll go to Halifax and we'll get married. I'd never give up Danny's baby—never."

Just before Christmas, she lost it.

"I never had such cramps, like the curse but ten times worse. And there was a clot, a rusty dark red clot. I looked at it, and before I flushed it away I thought of it being part of me and Danny, and I felt sad."

She was mad. Cracked. I told her so, but she ignored me.

"I may have a tipped womb like mom. She couldn't carry a baby. She had three miscarriages before me. Then she never got pregnant again."

The thought of Hettie Bennett even having sex—or taking part in any biological function, save a chaste, lemon-coloured daily pee—horrified me.

"You may not be thinking straight, Angie, but this is a good thing. You don't want people to say you had to get married. People don't ever forget that—not here they don't. It would start things off all wrong."

"They couldn't be more wrong anyway. It's not like he's one of the Irish professionals from the East End, although Mom would even object to one of them. It's that he comes from everything she looks down on: his religion, big family, drinking—everything. She'll never accept him or me marrying him. But I don't care. I wouldn't want to live without Danny."

Ma made a large Christmas dinner, and we had four Canadian airmen attend. One of them, who was quite tall and only nineteen, asked Ma if I was dating yet. This gave me a bit of a lift. But Ma said, "No. Dorothy has other things on her mind, like her studies." This was a real crock, but he didn't say anything to me after that. I thought that was mean of Ma, as I would have been happy to have someone to go to the show with, perhaps even to go skating and dancing with. I'd never even been kissed. Sometimes I felt really lonely, especially when I saw Angie and Danny so much in love.

On New Year's Eve, Angie and I were sitting on our sofa before the Christmas tree. Ma and Pop had gone to Watch Night at Gower Street United to sing hymns and pray for peace in the new year. Angie had dropped out of the Anglican choir, where she'd been a soloist. Hettie told Ma she feared "evil influences" were behind it. I suspected she was just anxious and depressed, and put off by the way Hettie was about religion.

"Danny's not religious," Angie explained, "but he gave me a St. Anthony medal. He said he liked St. Jude best—he's the saint for hopeless cases. Mom says Catholics pray to idols, but I once went inside the basilica and I thought it was really pretty, with stained-glass windows, statues of saints, and the Virgin Mary. Do you believe, Dottie, that there's something after you die? I'd like to see Grannie Bennett again. She used to comb my hair and take out all the tangles. Mom never had the patience."

"Jesus came to give us everlasting life," I said, with the authority that came from hearing endless sermons at Gower Street United since the age of seven, "but I'm not sure about it. Perhaps everything just goes dark, like turning off a light."

"I pray for Danny and me to be together. I even prayed for that little red clot, the beginnings of a baby, because Danny and I made it."

Then we stopped talking about religion and Angie did my nails, using the manicure set she had given me for Christmas. Outside, big flakes of snow came slowly down and surrounded the light pole that you could see from our front window. I tried not to think about Danny telling me to take care of Angie.

The Daily News had put out a special New Year's edition full of war news. The Germans attacked a convoy in the Barents Sea and we drove them off.

"Got the bastards on the run," said Pop.

"Any of our boys lost?" asked Ma.

"Doesn't look like it," Pop replied.

"Wouldn't it be a good thing if someone shot Hitler?" asked Ma.

"It sure would, Lou-Lou," said Pop, who only called Ma Lou-Lou, instead of Lil or Lillian, when he was feeling really playful. "Perhaps we should send you over with a machine gun under your new mink."

Pop had given Ma a mink coat as a Christmas gift, but Ma was afraid to wear it in case Hettie Bennett saw her in it. Hettie would say it was a slap in the face for Ma to wear anything but Newfoundland seal, this being wartime, and the local economy dependent on buyers.

"But so generous of your dear sweet Pop to do it," Ma said to me.

I strongly suspected that the gift was the result of guilt, as I noticed that Pop's new secretary, Ellie, laughed loudly at his jokes, some of which were really not that funny. I was at the office using her typewriter for an application for employment, an assignment for Miss Simmons, our English teacher. Girls were to apply as secretaries, boys as recent medical or law graduates.

Pop was also spending much more time at the office, where, Ma sighed, "Dear sweet Pop is working himself to death."

There was no divorce on the island, and it would really upset Ma. "Dear sweet Pop" would be toppled from his pedestal forever. So I would do what Pop always advised—I would "play it by ear" and "not worry about something I could do nothing about."

Angie's letters from Danny kept piling up. She kept them at my place in a locked jewellery box out of Hettie's eyes and reach. The mail was usually delivered around noon, and we arrived home from school at four-thirty, while Hettie didn't get home from the store until five. Angie would grab the mail and rush to her room.

"I know you understand, Dot, me wanting to be alone when I read them. It's just like he's here with me."

Danny was scheduled for a week's furlough at the end of March, and Angie was already making plans.

5. Man Down

IT WAS AFTER MIDNIGHT during the first week of February 1943. Pop was listening to the radio, which he kept on a table by his bed. I heard him go down to the kitchen and put the kettle on, and then I heard Ma, who'd probably been sleeping, join him. I walked from my room, sat on the stairs, and listened.

"There's a slaughter going on in the Atlantic, dozens of U-boats torpedoing our ships. Poor young bastards. There's not a chance in hell of any kind of rescue."

I was in the kitchen in a heartbeat. "What's the convoy number?"

Pop shrugged.

"You thinking of Angie's young chap?" asked Ma.

"It'll be in *The Daily News* tomorrow," said Pop.

I was grateful he didn't say not to worry about something I could do nothing about. I couldn't sleep.

The paper came. An estimated ten ships had sunk during the U-boat campaign in the Atlantic. There were no survivors. There were still some ships, but they were surrounded by U-boats waiting for darkness. The casualties consisted of many Nova Scotia and Newfoundland seamen whose names were yet to be released.

Angie didn't read the papers, so I didn't want to worry her if I could help it—although everywhere people were talking, and special prayers were said at school assembly. I asked myself if she was tuning out.

"Heard from Danny?" I asked her the next morning.

"Not for a bit. He said in his last letter his convoy was heading out. I can't wait for March." She smiled at me brightly in the winter sunshine as we walked the snow-packed sidewalks of LeMarchant Road.

The attack lasted for four days. By the end convoy SC-118 had lost thirteen ships, attacked by twenty U-boats. There were no survivors.

I had to tell Angie, but Mrs. Flaherty, Danny's mother, got to her first.

Seaman First Class Daniel Thomas Flaherty lost at sea Stop Feared dead Stop, the telegram said.

"You better get over here," Hettie said over the phone to me, her voice as cold as the icy Atlantic, where Danny's body was drifting downward. "You've been a part of all this with your lying and conniving. Now you can help your friend, or she's off to the Waterford for shock treatment."

I went next door. I saw Angie, eyes sunken in grey pockets.

"I want you to tell me there's been a mistake," she demanded. She was out of it. Then she burst into "We'll Meet Again," loudly and boldly.

"This is what happens when you deceive and lie," Hettie spat, opening the bedroom door. She was as irrational as Angie, hinting that somehow Angie's relationship with Danny had caused the German U-boats to torpedo him. "You've ruined yourself for any decent man."

"Get away from me. You called Danny a maggot, so he got killed to show you he wasn't. You killed him, you bitch. I wish you'd died and not him. Everyone hates you, *hates* you!"

I couldn't believe this was Angie, sweet kind Angie, who was always saying nice things and smiling. Clement Bennett was nowhere to be seen. Hiding, I suspected.

The night of February 7 was a long one. I got Angie out of the Bennett house and into ours, and Ma and I took turns trying to calm her down. "She needs nerve pills," said Ma, "but we've only got pain pills."

"Let's give her pain pills," I suggested. "She's in terrible pain."

"It's a different kind of pain," said Ma. "It's in her heart. Our pills won't work ... Pray to God, Angie. Ask Him to help you."

But Angie was beyond prayer, and beyond our feeble attempts at condolence. God had let her down, badly, and He could not make amends now.

The next morning *The Daily News* carried the names of casualties. Daniel Thomas Flaherty, Seaman First Class, was on page three, his sailor's cap tipped above his right eye, jaunty as all get-out with that crooked smile of his, as if he'd just won hundreds in a poker game.

"Don't let Angie see it," I warned Pop. "She doesn't really believe it."

But there she was, standing by the kitchen table, hand stretched out. Pop gave me a helpless look, and handed the paper over. She disappeared upstairs, and when I went up she was sitting silent on the edge of my bed, reading Danny's letters. She didn't even look up.

Hettie came to the door on her way to Bennett's Furs, her stiff grey permanent wave hugging her head, a seal-skin hat perched on top, her lips thin, compressed, and bloodless. She declined tea, saying she was already late and that she had to open the store. "I want you to tell Angela that I forgive her for all the dreadful things she said to me last night. I realize she was upset and didn't mean them. I've never had any thoughts but for Angela's own good. Sometimes things happen for the best. Of course, Angela will never believe that. I also forgive you, Dorothy, for your part in all this. No doubt you thought you were being a friend. Things could have been worse."

Then she was out the door, and into her heated Ford where

Clement Bennett sat behind the wheel, mute and obedient, patiently waiting.

"Strange woman," murmured Ma. "I really don't know how things could be worse. The boy's dead, and her daughter's destroyed. I suppose if he'd lived and they'd gotten married, in her mind that would have been worse. And to say 'things happen for the best.' Poor boy, dead at eighteen, drowned in the Atlantic all alone."

I started to cry, and Ma turned stern. "You'll be no help to Angela if you break down, Dorothy. You're made of stronger stuff. You've been much too involved in this, but you can't stop now. You must help her."

"That's what Danny said," I whispered.

"Oh, did he? Perhaps he had a premonition, poor young chap."

"I wonder how he got the first class. He wasn't stupid, you know. He was sort of smart in a different, street kind of way. Maybe he got it for winning at poker." Ma just looked at me, and I realized I was making no sense.

Upstairs, Angie was still sitting on my bed reading Danny's letters, tears running down her cheeks. She needed to share her grief. "We'll go visit Mrs. Flaherty, I'm sure she's broken up as well."

February in Newfoundland is cold, grey, and endless. The Flaherty's row house was halfway up the hill, and we trudged toward it slowly, exhaling white puffs of breath into the frozen air. I savoured the distraction of physical discomfort, my fingers and toes frozen and my cheeks stiff from cold. I linked arms with Angie, as I always used to do in the old days before Danny, vainly searching for words of comfort.

"I'm going to start smoking."

"Why?"

"Why not?"

A strange sort of memorial to Danny, I suspected.

All eight Flahertys were home, wide-eyed and solemn, except for the three- and five-year-old who were on the floor building some sort of wooden train track that they were fighting over.

Mrs. Flaherty was a heavy woman in her late thirties, with a freckled face and ginger hair that bore the remnants of an old perm. Her stout, unsteady fingers held a Royal Blend, which she stubbed out on her tea saucer when we walked into the living room. The other hand held a wad of toilet paper. She said, "stop it," and "smarten up," to the two youngest in a loud, but not unkind, voice. They seemed to be well behaved and appeared to be used to receiving orders. She couldn't have been more unlike soft-spoken Angie, or Danny for that matter.

She got up with some difficulty, and I saw she was pregnant. She put her arms around Angie, who immediately erupted in wailing.

"It's alright, me luv, time heals everythin'. It's the will of God, remember that. Danny thought the world of you, said he was goin' to marry you." Angie's wailing increased. When Mrs. Flaherty continued, it was as if she was talking to herself as well as Angie, and she spoke softly. "He was my first and best. Always gave me money, even his paper-route money and his poker money. He only kept a little back for his fags. He could handle his father after he had a few. He'd just say, 'Cut it out, Pa. Hit the sack and sleep it off.' And off he'd go." Mrs. Flaherty's eyes filled, and she patted the wad of toilet paper against them.

There were three framed pictures on the papered wall: the one of Danny in his uniform with the crooked smile and jaunty sailor cap that had been in *The Daily News*; a picture of the royal family with the King, the Queen, and Princesses Elizabeth and Margaret; and a picture of the Virgin Mary, who was exposing a bleeding heart with a little golden cross impaling it.

I heard the front door open.

"Is this the famous Angela Bennett?" The rasping voice was slurred and husky. It belonged to a substantial man with Danny's thick black hair and blueberry eyes, even a touch of his lopsided smile. His face was flushed, his eyes blurred, and he held onto his gut protectively.

"This is Angela, Danny's girlfriend, and her friend Dorothy," said Mrs. Flaherty. She glanced at us both, her face flushed, and she frowned at her husband.

"I know who she is: a beautiful girl. Danny used to say he'd marry her, and I'd tell him fat chance they'd let her marry the likes of him—a little nothin' Mick from the railway houses. But he seemed sure you would. Cocky little bastard, our Danny, but he was the first and the best. And now he's drowned, fightin' for bloody England, who never did nothin' for him or any of us. Jesus, what a waste." Mr. Flaherty's voice became hoarse, and I thought he might start to cry.

At that moment, a Mrs. Walsh from next door came in with a dish full of baked pork and beans, which brightened the kids up, and another woman arrived with two loaves of freshly baked bread. They touched Mrs. Flaherty on her shoulder and murmured, "Sorry for your loss, Peg."

"I haven't had the heart to cook," Mrs. Flaherty explained. "Bernadette, give the kids some beans an' some bread an' m'lasses." Bernadette, a teenager who resembled Danny, did as she was told.

I wanted to leave, but Angie followed Mr. Flaherty into the kitchen where he was leaning over the sink, his shoulders shaking. Plucking at his shirt sleeve, she said in a loud voice, "I want you to know, Mr. Flaherty, I was going to marry Danny as soon as I finished school. He wasn't just being cocky. He even gave me this ring."

Mr. Flaherty said, "Bless your little heart my darlin'— Danny had great taste." And they both stood in the kitchen holding each other, shaking with sobs.

"Angie, we have to go."

Then Mr. Flaherty said, "Would you like a drink, darlin'?" And he held up a bottle of rum.

Angie said, "No, just a cigarette."

And from then on, she smoked all the time.

6. The Year After

ANGIE AND I WALKED HOME from school in silence during the frozen spring of 1943. I missed our old times together, when we used to laugh and nudge each other. I thought of how Danny would carry her books, but I never mentioned it. But she did. "Remember Danny carrying my books? No matter how cold it was he'd always come and carry them." I'd mutter, "I remember," not looking at her, but knowing she was crying.

I'd always go over on Saturdays, knowing she'd be alone, not that she ever spoke to Hettie. Sometimes she'd be in her bedroom reading Danny's letters. I'd go up the stairs and enter, and often she wouldn't even look up. I'd go over, place my arms around her, and beg softly, "There's a good show on—why don't we go?" On occasion she'd come, but she'd always ask, "Remember that first date, when Danny sang?"

Most often, she wouldn't be home, but I'd know where to find her. I'd head down to the cemetery and seek her out. There she'd be, head lowered, smoking her endless cigarettes, and slowly walking the narrow paths between the snow-covered tombstones. Her head would be uncovered, her coat open, her long tangled hair blowing in the harsh wind. "You'll get pneumonia," I'd scold, "freezing yourself to death." I'd button up her coat, pull up her hood, and rub her small icy hands. And even coax a small rare smile. I was doing what Danny had asked, but that wasn't why I was doing it.

The war in the Atlantic had started to change. In early March 1943, depth-charge mortars were fitted into the bellies of escorts for the first time. I wondered if this would have saved Danny. In May, nine U-boats were sunk in the mid-Atlantic in an attack that involved five convoys, and nearing the middle of May, forty-one U-boats were lost. By May 24 almost all U-boats were withdrawn from the North Atlantic.

"Too late for Danny," I said to Ma. "It's good Angie doesn't read the papers. Everything sets her off, as if she's raw inside. Sometimes I suspect she still doesn't believe Danny's dead, and expects to turn around and see him walking in the door."

The final exams were in June, and Ma and Pop wanted me to apply to Dalhousie in Halifax, or even McGill in Montreal. Education for girls wasn't taken seriously, and the current joke was that most girls were at university to work toward a MRS.

"You could teach, Dottie," Ma suggested, "or even get a library degree. Remember how you enjoyed that summer at the Gosling Library?" I had enjoyed it not just because of my reading, but because of all the servicemen coming in and talking to me. But I couldn't tell Ma that. And I couldn't leave Angie. An average student before she met Danny, she now had little chance of passing her last year. I would sit with her at our kitchen table, reading to her from the textbooks and asking questions, only to catch her staring into space, those huge green eyes seeing things I did not dare think about. I sympathized, but showing sympathy seemed to worsen her depression, so I finally became angry.

"Angie, you're going to fail your year, and you'll have to repeat, even if you only want to get into Commercial." Commercial was a one-year course consisting of typing, shorthand, and bookkeeping for grade-eleven graduates who were not going to university. It prepared you for secretarial and office work, and it was a prerequisite for employment for girls.

"I can't keep my mind on it," she murmured.

The prom was coming, and there were two invitations for Angie. No one had invited me. Most of my male classmates only reached my shoulder in any event. One of Angie's invitations came from Edgar Clarke across the street, who had obtained special permission to attend although he had dropped out years earlier. The other invitation came from a nice, dark-haired boy—a little like Danny—whose father owned a local gas station on Topsail Road. "Out of the question," she shuddered.

I had persuaded Pop to let me have the Lincoln, so on a Saturday morning in early June we drove to Pouch Cove, and sat on large rocks overlooking the Atlantic. Playful waves were scratching at the rock's granite roots and bursting into shreds of icy spaghetti-like foam. "I want to dive off these rocks, swim across the water, and meet Danny."

"It's been four months, and you're failing your year. You only knew Danny for six months. You can't mourn forever. What do you want to do?"

"Teach little kids. I'd like that."

"Then for God's sake pass your exams and go into early childhood education." Angie lit a Lucky Strike, inhaled, and looked out to sea with narrowed eyes.

"I'll try."

But it was too late, and she failed her year. I passed with first class honours, but I decided to go to Memorial, named in memory of our lost boys, for my first year. I needed to stay with Angie.

"Angie will survive without you," complained Ma. "You've no social life here. At Dalhousie you can make new friends, and Angie will be forced to have a social life as well. Edgar Clarke never takes his eyes off her. Hettie's beside herself, and Angie won't even talk to her."

I decided I would give her one year—I was afraid she'd

kill herself. There was too much talk about meeting Danny beneath the waves, and although I was ignorant of psychiatry, I suspected she was clinically depressed. I had looked it up at the Gosling Library and knew that it could result in suicide.

So I stayed. I attended two university socials where I wore a full three-quarter-length peasant skirt, ballet shoes, and a long-sleeved blouse with a large collar and black bow. My uncut hair was rolled up in front with the rest hanging dark and lank to my shoulders. I wore dark rose lipstick and watched everyone else jitterbug to "In the Mood." I had no dance partners.

And I tutored Angie.

She passed her year and applied for early childhood education. I went to Halifax and entered second year general arts at Dalhousie University.

"I'd have never made it without you, Dottie," she whispered to me the night before I left. "You know that. I wish you weren't going, but I guess I'll have to grow up."

"Danny told me to take care of you if anything happened. You've got to stop blaming your mother for his joining up. He told me he was going to join the navy before we met at Bowring Park. He was going to lie about his age. Then he met you and didn't want to leave."

"Why didn't you tell me this before?"

"You weren't ready." She still wasn't, and I should have known it. "It's not normal," I scolded, "to mourn this long. You're almost nineteen and becoming a teacher. Stop smoking—you smell like a truck driver. And start dating." She threw me a watery smile and blew her nose.

"You've been such a friend, Dottie, you know that. Don't know what I did to deserve you." I took her hand and gave it a squeeze.

"We'll stay in touch," I promised.

7. Meeting Wills

IT WAS SEPTEMBER 1944, and the war was turning around. During the first week of classes, Brussels was liberated, and by the end of September, Boulogne and Calais were freed by our troops. The end of the war was in sight, and there were already a few discharged servicemen on campus. One sat next to me in English and in Economics.

He was a bear of a man named William Campbell, with a mop of curly light brown hair, blue eyes, a square chin, and an easy grin. He had made sergeant before a shell had blown off his left kneecap in Normandy. He was twenty-five and had a sense of humour like Pop. The military was funding his education. After the first degree, he was heading for law school because, he said, "I began to realize how important justice was when I was in Europe." That was as far as he'd go about the war, but I knew he'd lost buddies, so I told him about Angie and Danny.

He was quiet for a minute, and then shook his head. "Poor girl. Perhaps she'll never really get over it. They never had any of the ups and downs you have going through ordinary life; just the high points, the love—and then the loss. It's terrible what war does to people: kids with no dads, wives with no husbands. The worst part happens when they lose them very young. Then there's always this vacuum, this black hole that they can't fill up, only with the fantasies of what might have been."

At this point I took his hand—which was rough, warm, with a brush of gold on the back—and squeezed it, and then we went out for coffee. The next weekend we drove to Dartmouth, where he introduced me to his mother, who was quiet and welcoming, and who was living on his dad's pension. His dad, he told me, had died of a heart attack at fifty-seven while Wills was overseas.

On the way back, he asked me up to see his apartment on Ingles Street, which he shared with a buddy who was away that week. I stayed the night. We had sex—my first time—using a military-supplied condom. "Left over from my time in service," he said. I didn't ask for details. I only cared that I loved his smell and his gentleness, and that I felt so complete when I nestled against his large frame. I knew he was pleased he was my first lover, although he teased me about it. I surprised myself with the way I loved pushing my nose against his neck, rubbing his back with my fingers, and giving him long wet kisses. And the shuddering excitement of the penetration. I thought of Angie. After that first time, I knew we'd always be together.

He said he never thought he'd meet anyone like me. I laughed and said my mother always said I had "redeeming qualities" but that I was a bit of a "maw mouth." He suggested that perhaps we should go through law school together so I could put my "maw mouth" to good use.

When I mentioned to Ma I was thinking of going into law, she didn't even reply. She just called Pop to the phone.

"What's this I hear?" asked Pop. "Women don't become lawyers; women become secretaries." I detected a tinge of pride, as well as humour, in his voice. I told him about Wills and that he was an ex-military sergeant and that we were serious.

"What does he think of this law business?" he asked.

"He suggested it."

Then he handed the phone over to Ma, who said, "She's

your daughter." I could tell Ma was shocked about my going to law school, but very pleased about Wills. Hettie had been hinting strongly that I'd be an old maid, and that perhaps my friendship with Angie wasn't "natural."

In December 1944, Angie started to go out on occasion with Edgar Clarke, who had been watching her from the other side of the Avenue for the last five years. His father finally died from cancer, and he was now the owner of Clarke's Printing, which was quite successful.

Edgar was sullen and pale, with straight dark brown hair swept back from a high forehead. He was a large man with a heavy dough-like body. He was about a hundred pounds heavier and a foot taller than Angie. I could never imagine them together—he was too humourless and controlling.

Angie wrote me long letters, seldom mentioning her parents, even though she still lived with them. When she did mention Hettie, I could tell their relationship was still strained, although her mother seemed to approve of Edgar, probably because he was considered a successful business owner. Angie loved her course, especially the practice sessions with the kindergarten kids, and she was looking forward to teaching full time. She wrote mostly about Edgar and his great devotion. He had loved her always, he said, and his gifts—a solid-gold watch, diamond clip-ons for her ears so expensive she feared wearing them, and even a brown seal jacket purchased from Bennett's Furs—were described in full. I thought these details were strange, but I couldn't put my finger on why.

I wrote her back, telling her about my relationship with Wills and cautioning her about acting too rashly, for perhaps the wrong reasons.

"He's buying her," I said to Wills.

"Guess he feels he has to."

"She always talks about his love for her, but never says she cares about him—never."

"Perhaps she doesn't."

"Then she shouldn't take his gifts."

"That's what I love about you, your integrity. Will you be returning my Christmas gift after you decide I'm not up to your standards?"

"It depends what it is."

He'd been worth waiting for, Wills. He was so smart about life. Of course, he was six years older than me and had been through the war. He came home with me that Christmas, and we brought his mother with us because he didn't want to leave her alone. She got along well with Ma, and it was all very proper with Wills and his mom staying at the Kenmount Motel. So we had a chaste Christmas, even after he slipped a platinum ring on my finger with a sapphire in the middle and two little diamonds on each side.

"Aren't you supposed to ask Pop, and then ask me to marry you while you're down on your one good knee?"

"I don't mind speaking to Pop, but I'm going to forget about the rest of the formalities. You know I've got a bum knee, and I'm taking you for granted." It was a real insult, but he laughed and gave me a light kiss on the top of my head when he said it. It was a beautiful ring, and later we'd manage to get together on New Year's Eve at the Kenmount to make up for our sexless Christmas.

Ma and Pop had an engagement party for us on Boxing night, the night after Christmas, and Angie and Edgar were there. Angie wore a long black dress with a plunging neckline. She had a cigarette steaming between her brown-tinged fingers, a line between her luminous green eyes, and a fixed smile. They stood somewhat apart from the rest of the guests, and Edgar towered over her, stolid and unsmiling. He did not budge from her side until she broke away, clearly exasperated, and said, "Dottie, can we go to the little girls' room?"

Once there, we looked at each other and laughed, and I felt

the warmth of our long-time friendship.

"So?" I didn't need to say more.

"So happy for you, luv. He's lovely, so nice and funny. He reminds me of your dad. What do you think of Edgar?"

"I hardly know him. I used to think he was a little weird, but sweetie, it's your choice. You've been unhappy for so long, I just want to see you feeling more like yourself. There's more to it than jewellery, and you're not a materialistic girl. I remember you at the Candlelight with that little ring that looked like it came from a crackerjack box, displaying it as if it were one of the Crown Jewels of London." I hadn't meant any harm, but Angie's face fell at the memory. "Angie, I don't think you're ready for a commitment. Perhaps you'll never be ready, but right now you're definitely not."

"They're not lining up at my door, you know. I've got a reputation for being unstable, and I hate living with Mom. I can't stand it. The only time I'm happy is when I'm teaching. Perhaps if had my own car full of kids, they'd take away the pain. Edgar never takes his eyes off me: I see him watching the house, checking on my every move. I don't know what he thinks I'm up to, but it makes me uneasy."

"Angie, please don't rush into this. It worries me."

"What'd you think of Edgar?" I asked Wills later. Wills shrugged.

"He won't let her breathe. All that public love—I never think it's the same in private."

I thought about what he said later. I had to remember this was from a man who'd given an engagement ring without even proposing. But still.

One more year and then law school. And I would be the first woman ever admitted to Dalhousie. It was scary, and I was thankful for Wills. In the meantime, we were taking advantage of our pre-law school period, taking walks hand in hand near the Halifax Harbour, eating at cheap fish restaurants, and going to parties with Wills's veteran friends. We even studied together. And we laughed a lot.

I phoned Angie on May 11, 1945. She had written to tell me that she would be a June bride. Edgar had prevailed. I was to be her maid of honour. I told her Wills and I were going to a VE Day celebration with all his old buddies, and I predicted a drunken brawl.

"I'm insisting on driving," I said. Wills overheard me and laughed.

"War's over in Europe, Angie," I said happily. Silence. Was I being insensitive? It had been two years. And I had assumed she was moving steadily away from the trauma of Danny's death.

"And Danny's not coming back." Her words were choked, as raw with grief as that first night.

"No sweetheart, he's not, and you're getting married next month." At this point Wills, who had been listening, walked by and touched my arm.

"Tell your little friend she's not ready to get married. This is not fair to her or to him."

I told her, but she said it was too late. Invitations had been sent out, and besides Edgar said he loved her enough for both of them. And the backseat of a car full of kids would take her mind off the past.

There were two hundred guests at the Anglican cathedral, all in formal attire, and there was a reception at the Old Colony Club. There was a five-course dinner, specially catered by a chef flown in from one of Montreal's finest restaurants. The bride was gorgeous, in her long white gown, with a flowing veil covering her mass of chestnut waves. She posed with a wide crimson smile beside the five-tiered cake, her imposing groom by her side, smiling for once. The only time she wasn't smoking was during the ceremony.

The night before the wedding, we had a rare chance for a chat. She was drinking, which was unusual. "Edgar has arranged for a cruise on the *Empress of France*. It's very expensive, and we've got an outside balcony suite. I told him it wasn't necessary, that so many places are in ruins, but he says Venice, Rome, and the Greek islands were left largely untouched, and we'll end up in Paris, which is still intact because of the surrender. Would you think I'm the world's worst bitch if I told you I'd settle for a one-room cabin overlooking the bay in Pouch Cove, with an outhouse and Danny Flaherty?"

She was lying on my bed. The window was open, and the slight fragrance of lilacs wafted through the open window, carried by the ever-present breeze. "Remember the night we danced in that little wooden gazebo next to the ocean and then all three of us looked at the moon?" She was still lovely at nineteen, with a face like a porcelain Madonna, framed by that chestnut mane, eyes greener than any eyes had a right to be. The cigarettes hadn't yet taken hold, but the pain seemed to have taken up permanent residence.

"I won't go down memory lane with you on the eve of your wedding. Try to think of positive things. You've got a man crazy in love with you, and you're going to see the world from a first-class cabin—you'll probably even sit at the captain's table. Tomorrow you're having a wedding to end all weddings, which will probably set your mother back thousands. You don't want to be hungover when you're opening those envelopes with big cheques—you know your guests will be so afraid of Hettie that they wouldn't dare give anything but big cheques." She permitted a brief smile, so fleeting as not to count.

"You and I know that none of this matters, not a rat's ass." That was all she said, but she caught her lower lip between her teeth, as she always did when thinking.

I didn't hear from Angie for a month. Wills and I decided we didn't want to wait until graduation; we wanted to get married at the end of August before starting our final year, the last year before starting law school. Married ex-servicemen got an extra monthly allowance. I was spending most nights at his Ingles Street apartment in any event, much to the annoyance of his roommate, who said we were "taking over."

"This is disappointing, Dottie," complained Ma. "We were more than willing to give you a wonderful wedding, just as good as Angela's. Guests would give you money, as we have done for so many couples. It would have been a good nest egg for you and Willy. You could have even put a down payment on a house."

I told Wills. He just turned his mouth down. He wasn't sold on a big wedding, although he probably wanted to make it up to me for never formally proposing and that wisecrack about taking me for granted, which I reminded him about every now and then. "It's up to you, Dots. I'm easy," he said.

So I thought of a compromise. "Ma, why not have a small family wedding with just a few cousins and neighbours and Angie as my matron of honour? If you and Pop want to, you can give us all the money you'd have spent on a big wedding." Ma wasn't happy, which meant Pop wasn't either—he told me his toast to the bride would have been talked about for years—but they reluctantly agreed.

Angie arrived home from her honeymoon in early July, seven weeks before our wedding. They never did get to Paris. She moved into Edgar's house across the street. His mother and sister had moved to a small apartment on Elizabeth Avenue. "Too close to Hettie," Ma whispered. Hettie was still next door, but business had slackened since the end of the war, and she was thinking of subletting Bennett's Furs to a seafood restaurant. The soldiers from Pepperell were leaving with half the town's girls, back to those places with all the glamorous names that might not turn out to be as glamorous as the new brides had hoped.

Angie did not look well. Her face had no colour, and her eyes were glazed. She told me little about the honeymoon except she had taken Danny's letters, and that Edgar had found and read them.

8. The Honeymoon

IT STARTED ON THE FIFTH DAY at sea, on our way to Venice. The *Empress of France* was a ship with every possible luxury, like a big floating hotel, so I decided I'd go to the spa for a massage and facial. Edgar said he'd wait in the cabin, or sit on the balcony and read, until I got back. I was gone for about an hour and a half, and I didn't even take the cabin key. When I got back, I knocked, but he wouldn't let me in.

He said he was busy reading, and then it occurred to me what he was reading. He was reading Danny's letters that I'd always kept locked in a special box. The key to that box was on the same ring as the key to the new car he had given me as a wedding gift, and I'd left it in the cabin. All those letters—there must have been fifty of them. Everything was in those letters.

I told Dot later, and she said, "Why would you carry letters from your past lover with you on your honeymoon? Why would anyone not crazy do something like that?"

I just liked to have them with me; it was like having a part of Danny close. I went to the bar, ordered a Manhattan, and had a few cigarettes. Some man, an elderly man with a goatee and an accent, tried to pick me up. I decided I'd tell Edgar I was sorry and that I'd get rid of them—I wasn't planning to get rid of them. I'd hide them somewhere else and would be more careful in the future.

I went back to our stateroom, but this time the door was

unlocked. Edgar was standing on the balcony with the letters, pitching them into the ocean. I begged him not to. But he kept throwing them into the ocean like little soiled seagulls. Then he said, "Now I know what a filthy little slut I married." He said worse than that.

He tore off my dress, ripped off my bra and panties, and threw me down on the bed. The sex we'd had before was never like that. I was yelling with pain, begging him to stop, but he wouldn't. He said he was going to erase every stain of Danny from me. He kept on and on, and I kept crying and yelling, and finally, when I started screaming, he came, as if my screaming really excited him.

After he left, I lay there on the narrow bed, looking at the waters of the Mediterranean glistening blue through the glass cabin doors, wishing I was dead. He came back. He'd been drinking. "You don't think I'm through with you, do you?"

It was worse this time. He pushed my face into the pillow so nobody could hear the screams. Then he said he'd punished me enough for that night, but that I had brought it all on myself. Then he left.

I had to get out of the cabin in case he came back, so I went to the bar, but I could hardly walk or sit down and there was a lot of blood. Then I went to sickbay and got some pain pills. I felt I'd been knifed between my cheeks. I went back to the cabin, and when he came in much later I pretended to be asleep.

The next morning, Edgar acted as if nothing had happened, but he said, "I knew about you and Flaherty. I used to follow you down to the cemetery. I even heard you singing together and watched a few times when he was screwing you on the graves. You know the happiest time of my life? February 7, 1943, when I saw his smirking face in *The Daily News* and realized he was gone, swimming with the fishes. Guess I was just as happy as Hettie Bennett, although I heard you cracked up and lost your year over a puke like that."

That day we were docked near Venice, and I was hurting and bleeding. "I'm in terrible pain," I told him.

He looked at me, smiled, and said softly, "Don't you think you deserved it?" I could see he was happy, happy to see me suffer. And this was a man who had sworn he'd loved me for years. Then he said, "Are you going to let this ruin our cruise? You'll never get another chance to see Venice." As if I'd caused it all.

I went on the excursion, but I could hardly walk. I was bleeding so much I bought some sanitary pads at the ship's dispensary before we left. Venice was so beautiful: gorgeous little alleyways, palaces and museums, restaurants and old ornate houses, up and down the canal. And the gondolas, so different and quaint. There was this strange light when you looked out to sea. And there I was, barely able to walk.

"I have to go back to the ship," I said. I could see he was annoyed, yet pleased that I was suffering. I was trying to make sense of all this. It seemed he'd already known everything that was in the letters. I couldn't understand the man he was revealing himself to be.

I saw the ship's doctor. He was an elderly man, retired from active practice, who I supposed had wanted an easier life. I was so embarrassed, but the pain overcame the embarrassment. I let him examine me. He gasped and said, "You need stitches. You're badly torn. I'm not a surgeon, but I can arrange to have you seen by an English-speaking friend of mine in San Marino." He didn't ask me questions, but he gave me pain pills and told me to go to bed.

That night there was a gala, and we were invited to sit at the captain's table. I was lying on the bed and I told Edgar, "I can't move. You go and say I'm sick."

"You know you brought this all on yourself. The captain hardly wants to look at *my* white skin and great tits during dinner."

After he left, I went out on the balcony and watched the

Venetian lights glimmering in the distance across the water. There was a haze over everything. I saw myself climbing over the railing of the balcony, dangling there for a moment, and then letting go. I went back to have a last cigarette, and then I was too tired to get up, the pills were so strong. I slept. When I woke up, he was there. I felt him looking down at me.

We docked at San Marino the next morning. "I'm going to the hospital, and I don't want you there," I told Edgar.

He did not argue, and just said, "Watch your mouth."

Dr. Grotteria was expecting me. When he'd examined me, he sighed and asked, "Who did this to you, little girl?"

"My husband." Dr. Grotteria shook his head.

"This man has deliberately injured you with what I suspect is a sharp instrument. Now I must stitch you up and hurt you again, because I don't want to give you a general anesthetic as you're here on your own. I'll give you some very strong medication and be as gentle as I can. If you want to rid yourself of this animal, I'll give you a report describing your injuries." He also said I had signs of trauma in the genital area. He put in twenty stitches. It was painful, but nothing like the pain Edgar had given me. He gave me more narcotics, a painkilling salve, told me to sit in the bath for an hour a day, and gave me a laxative.

"There are men, twisted men, who enjoy the infliction of pain on an unwilling partner, especially before or during the sexual act. What this man has done to you is extreme. Some women can tolerate, or even enjoy, a playful, slightly hurtful, dalliance as a prelude to sex. This does not fall into that category. This was a deliberate injury, and I fear for your safety if you remain. These things often escalate with time."

I just nodded.

It was now noon. The stitches felt as if I had a dozen dead spider's legs between my cheeks, but the pills plus the salve had eased things. I walked around the streets of San Marino in a daze.

I went into a little church and sat gently in a pew in the cool air. People came in and out, and trays of candles flickered in the front. There were statues of the saints and one of Jesus hanging from his cross, blood pouring from his side and a crown of thorns on his head. I slid to my knees and asked him to help me get rid of Edgar.

I thought of Danny, and of how, if he were here, we'd walk hand in hand around the walled city and sit close to each other in sidewalk cafés. I felt so raw and choked.

I had lunch by myself, a small salad and pasta with a glass of wine. Under the umbrella of the table on the sidewalk *ristorante*, I was bathed in a pool of liquid air and indirect sunlight. Danny walked up the sidewalk toward me. He wore his white sailor suit, his cap perched in that jaunty way on the side of his black hair. He paused at the table and looked down at me. I whispered, "Sit down." He just smiled and walked away into the liquid warmth. I wanted to cry out "Don't go," but as I watched there was only the air shimmering like the waters of the Mediterranean when the sun shines on it.

Edgar had planned our time in Rome: there were excursions to the Gallery at the Borghese Gardens and the Vatican. I had watched while he enthusiastically discussed these day trips with the ship's tour guide, portly in his vanilla-coloured linen suit and narrow-brimmed straw fedora. I found it strange he could show such animation, as he was so sullen when we were alone. I wanted to go home.

I arrived back at the ship around two. Edgar was furious. He told me I was a liar, that I hadn't even seen a doctor and I'd exaggerated my so-called injuries to gain attention and to get away from him. He insisted I show him the stitches. We were in our cabin, and across the water the brown Mountains of

San Marino were baked against the hard-blue sky. I thought maybe if he saw what he'd done he'd realize how much he'd hurt me. I started to shake as I lay on my side, facing away from him, not trusting him not to touch me. He asked when we could have sex again. I started to cry. I could feel his fingers rubbing against the stitches. I turned and looked at his face, and I could see it was exciting him.

I was in a haze for the rest of the cruise, taking the maximum dosage of pills Dr. Grotteria had given me. Although I was exhausted, I hardly slept, and I felt him watching my every movement, even when he thought I was asleep.

It was the final night gala, and Edgar had assembled a special table of dinner and bar companions he had met during the cruise. I refused to go to Paris, so we were heading home the next day. I watched him as he carefully combed his straight dark hair, patted aftershave on his full pale cheeks, and slipped into his midnight blue tuxedo, purchased, he had told me, especially for the cruise. "Well?" He was standing in front of me, stout but elegant.

"You look ... very nice."

"Only very nice?"

"Handsome, like a movie star."

"That's better."

There had been no further violence, but I was always waiting. It had been, I hoped, a once-in-a-lifetime occurrence.

"You're wearing that black gown?"

"Yes."

"Change it. It's a festive occasion; there's no need to look as if you're going to a bloody funeral. Wear your blue—it'll go with my tux."

Edgar was a generous host, ordering bottle after bottle of champagne, and having the table laughing when he imitated an Italian speaking English with a strong accent. "Your husband's so jolly, such absolute fun," gushed Adele Young, a woman who was heading back to London with her solicitor husband. I smiled. Edgar had been filling up my glass all evening, and I was feeling lightheaded.

On the way back to the cabin, I was a little clumsy, and Edgar placed a steadying hand on my elbow. After we entered the cabin, I started to undress, but then became aware of his sitting, watching me. "You know you drank too much," he said.

"But you kept filling my glass."

"Because you were gulping it down." He smiled, lit a cigarette, and leaned back in the cushioned chair. "You have to be punished, you know that. I can't have my wife acting like some cheap little drunk."

I felt my hands go numb, and my body tense. The five-course dinner and glasses of champagne pressed against my throat. I rushed to the washroom and threw up. I heard his voice continuing through the half-open door: "You won't be able to escape what you deserve by doing that."

9. Homecoming

B Y THE TIME WE ARRIVED home, I was scared of Edgar. The chance of pain was always lurking. Dottie phoned, but I would only speak to her briefly, refusing all invitations to visit. I knew he might phone, as he did every hour when he was out of the house, always saying he was "just checking in." And if I was on the phone when he called there would be another reason for him to punish me, although by now I knew that no reason was needed.

I'd prepare dinner and eat before he got home. He would eat slowly, watching me, watching my shaking hands. "You know the drill." His voice would go a little higher, and he'd moisten his lips with his tongue.

"I didn't do anything," I'd always stammer, but there was always something: I'd taken too long to answer his call, the dinner was not hot enough, or I was too slow in bringing it to him.

"You must behave," he'd say, "then it wouldn't be necessary." He would say it in a soft, high voice, but his fingers would be restlessly tapping the table, as if he couldn't keep them still. "You know the drill."

I would go up the stairs to the bedroom slowly, take off my clothes, and place them on top of the bureau. Then I'd sit on the edge of the bed and wait. I would hear the heavy tread of his work boots as he came up the stairs. He'd never undress. The chair by the bed was large, and he would sit there and pat his knees for me to lie across them. Above the chair, the crystal chandelier would glitter.

"If you did as you were told, I wouldn't have to do this."

I waited for the pain to start. After he was finished, he'd stand there watching me, eyes narrowed, a dull flush on his pale cheeks and a glaze of sweat on his forehead. "Let this be a lesson to you," he'd say softly. Then in his normal voice, "There are other things I'll be doing to you. You must try to adjust, to make friends with the pain." I thought of the magazines in the basement, with the naked women tied to chairs.

It was then that I started to withdraw into my own safe crystal world, nestled in the bright lights of the chandelier, where there was no pain and I was secure, wrapped in my white bright igloo. Edgar hated it. The slapping became harder and lasted longer. But I was not responding. "You're playing games with me," he said, "and it's going to stop." I knew what was behind his words: I had not been crying out. I was living in the bright light of my crystal palace, and it protected me. "You'll still get your spankings—I'm working on that little ass of yours—but there'll be other things. I've been much too kind, and you've taken advantage."

Each night, the now-naked stallion removed me from my crystal world to the living room's rough carpet where, on my hands and knees, I'd await the mounting for my ride around the track. He rode me hard, spurred on by my screams until he withdrew, leaving a weak and silent filly. Hating the silence, he'd start again, using his mouth and hands, seeking out the vulnerable and hidden parts till a flick from his tongue would cause me to cry out. Then he'd torment and degrade me with his gadgets. I hated him but not as much as I hated myself. I let him do too much. "I have to leave you," I sobbed one night, after hours of pain and humiliation.

"And where will you go?" he asked softly. "Do you want me to tell Hettie what her slut daughter lets me do to her, or talk to your friend Dottie?"

I lived on the few of Dr. Grotteria's pain pills that remained, and I used creams and compresses during the day to lessen the damage from the night before, knowing that each night Edgar would start again.

I knew I'd have to cancel the pre-kindergarten teaching position I had starting in September. He'd even go with me for groceries, and he'd check on me at home by phone throughout the day. If I didn't pick up at once, I'd have to be "punished."

I thought of escape, but shame kept me there. I'd let him do it. Did I feel I deserved the pain because I married him when I still loved Danny? Or did I feel the physical pain would take my mind off the other pain, the pain always present in my heart? Was I that crazy? I longed to tell Dot, but she'd confront him, I knew she would. Then if I couldn't get away, things would be worse.

One night, during the first week of August—a month after we returned from our so-called "honeymoon"—I got out of bed hurting so bad I couldn't sleep. I took two of the pain pills Dr. Grotteria had given me and saw there were only six out of the sixty left. I wondered if I was addicted, but I really needed them for pain. I poured a few ounces of Edgar's Crown Royal into a tumbler, took my cigarettes, and went out back. I sat on the cement steps facing our backyard, waiting for the pills to kick in and hoping the rye would hurry it up.

It was a warm August night, with far-off pinpricks of stars and a hazy, scarred moon. I breathed in the sharpness of our cedar hedge and the strong sting of the spruce. Hopelessness sat like a grey blanket, heavy around my shoulders. I thought of getting in my car, driving up Signal Hill, and speeding off the cliffs, flying like a giant metal seagull over the waters of the Narrows, and then diving down to where Danny was waiting. I struggled with this impulse, but, as on the ship, the pain pills were kicking in and draining me.

Then I felt a surge of hope, like a veil lifting. I would leave Edgar. I had let him degrade me, but I wanted to believe I was still of some value. I'd fly to Toronto, or Montreal, and get work there—anything to do with children. I'd try to start again. Perhaps I could be a nanny or work at a daycare. I could even sing at night in a club. I thought of going to Halifax, where Dot would be, but Edgar would track me down.

I'd pick my time, but it had to be soon. I'd withdraw five hundred dollars from our joint account with the Bank of Nova Scotia, where Edgar also kept the Clarke Printing account. I'd take just one suitcase—I wanted nothing from him. The thought of freedom, combined with the pain pills and alcohol, gave me a heady feeling, and my physical pains and depression became less.

I'd write a letter to Mom on the day I was leaving, telling her of my unhappiness, and that I was going to Canada to start a new life. I'd tell her nothing more.

I'd also leave Edgar a letter, begging him not to try to find me. This was what I feared most. I'd also tell him there was no one else. I was afraid he'd jump to this conclusion, even though it made no sense as he watched over my every breath and move.

Dottie was working at her father's office all summer and living at her mom and dad's place with Willy. They were getting married this month, and I was to be her maid of honour. I had to leave, but I knew she'd be hurt, as she probably already was, by our lack of contact. I couldn't leave at night, and I didn't encourage her to visit, with Edgar listening to and monitoring my every word. He always associated her with Danny. I would phone her tomorrow and somehow meet with her. But I couldn't tell her what was happening; I was so ashamed.

"I won't be home for lunch," Edgar said the next day. "Good chance for you to get some rest—you're not lookin' good."

"Wonder why?" I muttered.

"Gotta toughen you up," he said, giving my breast a sharp squeeze and smiling as he saw me flinch.

You don't want to toughen me up. It's no fun without making Angie cry out.

"Hello stranger," said Dottie, her voice sounding both hurt and annoyed when I phoned. "Why one o'clock? We're across the street, and I've got clients coming in during the lunch hour to sign up for real estate closings. I'll come between two and three. God knows why."

She was standing in our living room at two-thirty, her dark straight hair pulled back, anchored by an elastic band, tall and slim in her navy suit and white blouse. Her dark eyes behind her horn-rimmed glasses were looking at me intently, and she was scowling. "You look awful, Angie. Are you alright? Not pregnant, are you?"

"No Dot, nothing like that. I'm leaving Edgar, but no one can know. Promise me. Someday I'll tell you more, but not now."

"He's not hurting you, is he?"

"No."

"You'll miss the wedding."

"You've got to forgive me, Dottie."

She came over and put her arms around me, and I started to cry. I'd missed her so much. I wanted to tell her everything but I couldn't. I'd phone her from Montreal.

Edgar came home early in a foul mood. His luncheon had not gone well, and his baked fish was still in the oven. Worse, he'd phoned while I was seeing Dot to her car, and I hadn't picked up.

"Why didn't you pick up?"

"Dot dropped by; I was seeing her off."

"Why'd she drop by in the middle of the afternoon?"

"She had to pick up something at the house, and she wanted to tell me more about the wedding."

"Strip."

"Edgar, no one was here but Dot."

"Strip."

I did as I was told. He examined me: a rough penetration with those sturdy strong fingers, and then an examination of my bruised bum. "I think I'll add a few new ones tonight. Gotta smarten you up and show you who's boss."

It was useless to try to fight him. I let him do what he wanted, which was a twenty-minute spanking before the ride around the track. It was his last hurrah, but I didn't cry out enough, so there were some extras. Tomorrow night I'd be safe in a hotel room in Montreal. Blissfully alone.

10. The Flight

The flight for Montreal was leaving at noon, and the taxi was picking me up at ten forty-five. I withdrew five hundred dollars from the bank at ten, and then I left my letter for Mom in her mailbox, and Edgar's on the kitchen table.

The taxi was early. The driver took my one bag—I'd left a closet full of clothes—and gave me a broad smile. I noticed a missing tooth and a flushed face. A drinker, I thought, but a pleasant one—probably until he got into the booze. "Off to Toronto?"

"Yes." I wouldn't say Montreal—Edgar might be making inquiries.

"Too bad we might have to join 'em, but maybe best in the long run."

I'd taken a painkiller. In a few weeks my body would stop hurting. The city shone at me through the taxi window as we made our way past the brightly painted wooden houses and the occasional estate, far back from the road, with a gravel pathway lined with large maples. The taxi bumped over the cobblestones of Water Street, passing a red streetcar rattling on its tracks. "They're gonna pave Water Street an' get rid of the streetcars—tryin' to keep up with Canada."

"So I hear."

I opened the car window, breathing in the harsh fresh air from the harbour for the last time as we passed the two-storey department stores on Water Street. I thought of that night with Danny by the water in the back seat of Mr. Butler's Lincoln, so long ago. Layers of heaviness had started to lift, and I felt a stirring of hope. But I was nervous. I knew I would be until I was on the plane.

I pictured Edgar coming home and finding me gone. Would he come after me? I'd change my name and go back to Europe. He'd never find me there. But I'd taken only five hundred dollars. I should have gotten more money from Dot. I had my passport. I'd go to Italy where I'd teach English.

We drove by the Newfoundland Hotel, past the large mansions on Circular Road, and then past miles of spruce-lined highway. My cold hands were trembling. I looked at the large diamond on my ring. Perhaps I could pawn it in Montreal. My heart was fluttering with fear and excitement as we approached the airport. In another hour I'd be flying away from Edgar Clarke. Forever.

The taxi stopped directly in front of the entrance. The driver deposited my bag next to me and smiled when I tipped him. I'd learned about tipping from the big tipper Edgar. "Good trip, ducky."

I nodded my thanks and walked slowly toward the doors, the weight of the suitcase tipping me to one side. A hand reached down and took the handle.

"Might as well turn around now," he said. His other hand tightened around my arm as he steered me toward his car in the parking lot. For a second I thought of running, leaving the bag, and attempting to board the plane. He read my mind. "I cancelled your flight, said you were suddenly taken sick. They had others on stand-by. Seems I got friends here, helpin' me keep an eye on you. Bill Kendrick, the bank manager, phoned as soon as you made that withdrawal. He wanted to check and see if I knew about it. I made like I did—no need to expose you as a little thief.

"Then there was another call—your mother Hettie. Seems you left her a goodbye note—no details though. Seems like she doesn't know what her slut daughter lets me do to her. She wondered if we'd 'had a little spat,' and she 'wanted to stop Angela from doing something impulsive that she'd regret later on.'" His voice, imitating my mother, was taunting.

I felt my throat swell with rage. Another betrayal.

Nothing happened. He stayed home the rest of the day, and he watched me, but he didn't touch me. I heard him phone my mother and thank her for saving the marriage. "You may want to phone Dot Butler and tell her you've cancelled your plans. Surprised she didn't help you like she did with Danny."

I took another pain pill. I would get more from Dr. Macpherson tomorrow. I never knew when I'd need them. But Edgar didn't touch me. Not for ten days.

11. The Attack

WHEN I CAME TO, there was a cold cloth on my head and an ice pack under my bottom. It was one o'clock. Edgar stood next to the bed. He said I'd been out cold for about thirty minutes and he'd been getting worried.

My muddled thoughts went back to what had happened. I'd been at the cemetery last Friday and had spoken to his mother and sister, who were tending the Clarke plot. His mother must have mentioned this to him during one of their rare phone calls, and it triggered his crazy jealousy, as he'd always associated the cemetery with Danny. He'd come home, dragged me from the shower, and beaten me with Granny's hairbrush. Then when I'd stopped yelling and started drawing away in my mind, he used the long wooden handle. I could feel what he'd done. There was a sharp pain, and I could feel something warm, and I knew it was blood, seeping from inside.

After I came to, I whispered, "Edgar, you're sick. I have to leave you because you're crazy and you'll end up killing me."

"You don't mean that. You know you don't mean that."

"Yes, I mean it. It doesn't matter what anyone thinks anymore."

"I can't live without you. I'll kill myself if you leave. It's not my fault I get carried away. It's my mother—she screwed me up. I do love you, you must know that." He placed his face in his hands and started sobbing, harsh deep sobs.

"You don't know about love, Edgar. You only know about pain."

He kept crying, telling me how sorry he was, kissing my hand again and again. He told me he'd help me have a baby. He knew I wanted a baby. He said he wouldn't touch me for nine months if the doctor recommended it. I could stay in bed and he'd bring me meals, even cook them. He said he'd make it up to me in a hundred ways. I felt nothing, just numb.

"I don't trust you."

It was Monday, and Dot's wedding was on Saturday afternoon. I was bleeding and in pain. I knew I should see a doctor, but I was too embarrassed and ashamed.

I couldn't get up. The only relief was when I took painkillers—the kind I'd had in Italy, that Dr. Macpherson had refilled weeks before—and when I had ice cubes on my bottom. Edgar kept hovering around, getting me ice. I couldn't look at him.

It didn't ease up. When I finally got up to pee, it felt as if I were passing acid. But I was determined not to miss Dot's wedding.

On Wednesday, I took a handful of pills and went to the dressmaker for a final fitting. She glimpsed my bruises right through my panties and asked, "What happened to you?"

"I had a bad fall," I said. She just looked at me strangely.

I visited Dot on Friday night and told her about the honeymoon, and the letters, and about Edgar's jealousy, although I didn't go into details. She said she'd help me leave.

On Saturday, I went to the church. It was a beautiful ceremony. Dot looked so tall and graceful, and I saw the way she and Wills looked at each other. I was glad for them but sad when I thought of my own marriage.

12. Some Revelations and a Wedding

IT WAS THE WEEK OF THE WEDDING, and I finally got together with Angie, saying that we had to discuss the details of the ceremony. I noticed Edgar watching from his veranda when I opened the front door. Angie came in and slouched in the softest chair, a cigarette between her fingers. She appeared in pain, her eyes dull and half closed. She seemed drugged. She related what I believed was only part of her honeymoon experience: Edgar's reading of Danny's letters and the rough sex. He had caught her at the airport three weeks before.

"You should try to leave him again."

"I can't fight him or refuse him. He loves pain—my pain. And I'm always late," she murmured, "but I don't carry it. I have the usual cramps, and he wants sex all the time. You won't tell Willy any of this, will you?"

"You're worrying me to death. Angie, please think about leaving him again. You'll have to let me help you this time."

I couldn't resist telling Wills as soon as he arrived home. He was assisting at the Department of Justice for the summer, believing it would ensure his admittance to law school, and sleeping on Ma and Pop's sofa, which was one reason for the August wedding. Our intimate moments were spent in the back of Pop's Lincoln, which always made me think of Angie and Danny.

"It's really awful," I told Wills, "and I sense she's only told me part of it. I know her so well, and she always looks away when she's hiding something. No wonder they didn't go to Paris."

"He's a sick fuck, really sadistic," said Wills, "though you have to ask yourself what she's doing, carting around old love letters on her honeymoon. But you can't treat someone like that. What's she doing staying with him? She's a gorgeous girl, but a little clueless. Why's she staying with a sick weirdo like Edgar Clarke?"

"I love her: she's sweet and kind, and she always had a sense of humour. On some level, she believes she should be punished for marrying him. She's not even twenty, but she looked awful tonight. She seems to think if she has children everything will be all right. In that way, you could say she isn't thinking. Danny called her a little girl, but she's much more than that."

Our wedding took place at the end of August with Angie, looking drugged and lifeless, as my matron of honour. There were twelve wedding guests, including Hettie and Clement Bennett. Edgar claimed to be sick. I suspected he knew that Angie had confided in me and he at least had the decency to be embarrassed. Or perhaps he just disliked me.

Ma arranged for a sit-down turkey dinner at the Brigus Tea Rooms, fifty miles out of town. We were toasted with champagne, and Ma and Pop presented us with a cheque for fifteen thousand dollars—a huge amount of money in 1945. It was enough to pay for a house in Halifax. We'd rent the first floor out to students, keeping the upper floor for ourselves. Angie had left the dinner early saying that she was unwell, and everyone thought she was pregnant.

Our honeymoon in late August was spent driving around the dusty roads of the island, stopping off at bed and breakfasts, and looking at the waves. The night before our return to Halifax, Angie came to say goodbye.

"It's good to see you looking so happy, Dottie. Remember

how I used to tell you that you'd be tall and beautiful when the rest of us were gone to pulpy seed? And he's a lovely man. You always complained about men who only came to your shoulder, remember?" She was in my bedroom. I took the cigarette from her fingers and flushed it down the toilet. "You'll have a face full of wrinkles, and it's not good for you. Give it a break." But before I had the words out, she was lighting up again. "It doesn't matter. It really doesn't. I don't like Edgar, and he knows it. In fact, I hate him. I do all the usual things: cook, clean, iron his shirts. Even gave up my job, the only thing I really enjoyed. I get pregnant, and then lose it because of Edgar. We're going to Montreal next week to see an obstetrician, and I also need some repair work done. I'm going to have a baby even if I have to stay in bed for nine months with no sex. Edgar promised me that." I sat speechless, looking at her, my mouth open.

"Angie, I thought you were leaving him. Don't you remember that I said I'd help you? Why this crazy rush to have a baby? We're going to wait until I'm finished law school and then some. The world is starting to change for women."

"I'm not clever, Dot. Not like you. Ever since Danny I'm empty, and a baby will fill me up. I might even start liking Edgar if he was good to the baby." She was damaged. And she was talented. I thought of the laughs and talks we had together in the old days, long before Danny and Edgar.

"Angie, you're making a terrible mistake. Leave Edgar— he's sick. Go back to teaching. And in time try to have a nice balanced relationship—like Wills and me—with someone who'll love you in a normal way." She bit her lower lip, those luminous green eyes of hers gazing into the distance, still lovely in spite of the grey smudges beneath them and the line between her eyebrows.

"You don't really understand, Dot, and I hoped you would.

It really doesn't matter who I'm with if I'm not with Danny. It could be anyone."

She was right. I didn't want to understand.

13. The Eleven Good Months

W E WENT TOGETHER to see Dr. Gervais at the Montreal General. He was the top man: a surgeon, a gynecologist, and a fertility specialist. I went in first, and I told him a lot. "With Edgar," I told him, "it always hurts."

Dr. Gervais examined me on his table in his office, and said he suspected I had a tear in my uterus which had to be repaired before I could even think about becoming pregnant.

"Uterine tears are dangerous," he said, "and can result in a ruptured womb during childbirth. This can be fatal for both mother and child."

I got furious with Edgar all over again.

Dr. Gervais was a lovely man, quite handsome, and he didn't give me the usual "little girl" label. He leaned back in his chair and looked at me with narrowed brown eyes.

"Do you enjoy the pain your husband gives you?"

"No, Dr. Gervais. I don't like being hurt, but my husband says he'll do everything you tell him because I told him I was leaving. He said that the rough sex will stop."

"Do you believe him?"

I didn't answer.

"I suspect you don't," he said. "I'll have to repair the tear in any event, and there'll be no sex for two months. At that time, if you're still with this man, we'll talk about a pregnancy. I urge you to get rid of him. Your husband's conduct is cruel, sadistic, and extremely dangerous. He needs psychiatric help." Then he told me to get Edgar so he could talk to him alone.

Edgar was in the doctor's office for at least half an hour, and when he came out he was fuming. "You really spilled your guts to that bastard," he growled.

"No," I said, "I didn't tell him half."

Dr. Gervais really scared Edgar. In spite of everything, he didn't want to lose me, and Dr. Gervais had really put this fear into him. The doctor had told him that the damage done was the sort a woman experiences while giving birth.

We went to a small French restaurant around the corner from the hospital after we left. Edgar didn't speak while we walked, he just kept his head down, but then, after we got shown to our table, he ordered his Crown Royal, looked right at me, stretched out his hand, touching my arm, and said, "I went way too far that day. I don't know how you'll ever forgive me for what I did."

I didn't answer him; I only took a sip of wine and looked away. I didn't trust him. Dr. Gervais informed Edgar he'd told me to leave, which was another worry.

"Gervais," Edgar complained, "went way beyond just fixing your womb."

"The doctor said no sex for two months after surgery, and after this, if I get pregnant, no sex for nine months. Can you promise that?" I asked him. I was feeling powerful for the first time in the marriage.

"I'll do like he says," Edgar said softly.

"Sometimes your promises mean nothing," I told him.

After the repair, I stayed in hospital for a week, and Edgar was there every day, even though Dr. Gervais never spoke to him. He bought me flowers, chocolates, face cream, even a fancy blue nightgown with a little lace jacket. The nurses thought he was wonderful and asked me what I'd done to deserve such a loving husband.

After I was discharged, we stayed at the Windsor Hotel.

We went to some fine French restaurants, and he bought me expensive clothes at Holt's, although I insisted it was unnecessary.

I'd watch the two of us reflected in the store windows on St. Catherine's Street. Edgar was so big, with his dark suit and black sunglasses, towering above this little flea with a big head of hair beside him. He'd always take my hand and I looked like his little girl, although he was only two years older.

I kept waiting for something to happen. We'd lie in bed together, and he'd feel me all over. Then he'd leave, go outside, and walk around the sidewalks of Montreal. I knew there were prostitutes around, so I'd say, "Did you meet anyone?"

"Wasn't looking," he'd reply, and I'd feel bad for asking.

Once he rubbed his finger on my clit and said, almost sadly, "Poor little joy button, put through so much." I felt like saying, *And whose fault was that*? But I didn't.

After we went home, he left me alone as promised. Often he'd go downstairs to the basement, and I suspected he was pleasuring himself with his dirty magazines.

I once asked him if I could do anything to help. He was lying next to me, and he had a full erection. I said, "I could just rub some nice hand lotion on it and perhaps it would feel better." He just laughed and said he wasn't into anything I'd do, but that he appreciated the offer. I said, "This is hard on you."

He answered, "Not as hard as losing you would be."

After two months we went back to Montreal to see Dr. Gervais. He said the tear had healed nicely but couldn't withstand the previous "savage onslaughts." Dr. Gervais certainly had a way with words, and he always succeeded in upsetting Edgar. "If Mrs. Clarke is to be impregnated," he ordered him, "you'll have to rein in your uncontrolled roughness. When she does become pregnant, there'll be bed rest and no sex for nine months."

"Gervais is probably hung like a pencil," Edgar muttered

as we left the hospital, "and I suspect he's interested in you."
Edgar and his crazy jealousy.

That night at the Windsor Hotel, we had sex for the first time
in over two months. He couldn't have been more concerned
and solicitous. I actually felt a slight twinge of pleasure, and
at the end I asked, "Did you get anything out of it at all?"

"It's not about me," he replied, and I started to care for
him, but I still didn't trust him.

After a week in Montreal, we flew home. I got pregnant
right away. Of course, getting pregnant wasn't the problem:
it was staying pregnant. I stayed in bed, and he brought me
meals. Some he'd pick up from local restaurants, others he'd
get from Hettie, although we were barely speaking. He even
cooked a few basic things like steak and fried cod himself.
He'd bring the dishes on a little tray with a vase with one
flower he'd pick up at Tessier's Florists. He'd even printed
a small engraved card at the printing shop that said, *Angela
Clarke, Mommy-in-Waiting*, that leaned against the vase. It
was a side of him I hadn't seen since the wedding.

He'd bring me in a basin of hot water so I could wash, then
he wanted to wash me. "Can I trust you?" I'd ask him.

"Sure you can trust me," he'd say softly.

He'd wash and dry every bit of me, even examining me
down below as if he were a doctor. He'd rub scented cream all
over me, feeling everything. Then he'd disappear downstairs.

"It makes me hot," he explained.

"Would you rather not do it?" I asked.

"You're kidding. It makes my day."

I suggested having a hairdresser come once a week to
shampoo. There was one available who went to the hospitals,
but I was treading on his territory. He would shampoo my
hair, using two basins, those thick strong fingers of his
massaging my scalp with Halo shampoo, then the rinse, the
towel dry, the comb out—a tedious procedure that took him
hours. "You're like Grannie Bennett," I teased. "She used to

take out my tangles. Mom didn't have the patience."

"Believe me, I'm no Grannie Bennett," he said, smiling.

Edgar would bring me things, but never perfume because he said he loved my smell, even if it was smoky at times. He even bought me dark pink nail polish and put it on after he'd given me my bed bath. He had these large hands and thick fingers with little black hairs like wires on the back, and it was so funny to see him apply polish with those clumsy-looking hands. I'd say, "You don't really need to do this, it's not as if we're going anywhere."

He'd look at me, really wounded, and say, "I want you to look beautiful anyway. Don't I count?"

And I'd say, "Sure you do." I was playing along with him in a sense, as I still couldn't trust him. I kept waiting for something to happen.

After he'd bring my tray down at night, he'd come upstairs, lie on the bed, and we'd listen to the radio together. It was a great radio, an Admiral Broadcast Band—Edgar always got the very best. We had access to out-of-island stations, and we'd listen to Jack Benny, Fred Allen, and Groucho Marx. Edgar loved Groucho. We'd listen to music; Frankie Laine and Frank Sinatra were big that year—of course, Sinatra stayed big. "You never sing anymore," Edgar complained. "When you were in high school I used to leave work and go to listen at morning assembly. You used to sing all those war songs. You could really sing. I want you to sing for me, not any of the crap you and Danny used to sing, but the songs we listen to."

"I can't sing anymore. My throat's smoked out," I told him. He kept pushing me, so I sang "Heartaches" for him. He loved it. He said my voice was "husky, mature, and sexy." Then I sang "Mean to Me." I thought it had a special significance.

"You could have been a professional singer, but now you can only sing for me," was his comment. He really loved music, but he couldn't carry a tune. He liked very dramatic stuff, like "All of Me." Strange for a man like Edgar.

He started bringing home magazines: *Good Housekeeping, The Ladies' Home Journal*, that sort of thing. Then he started to bring me *The Daily News* every morning on my breakfast tray. At first I just read the marriages and deaths, but later I started to read the whole paper. It was very interesting. Dottie used to say, "Angie, you've got to read the newspaper. They're more people in the world than just you."

Reading it, I realized that I didn't know anything. I thought about Venice and Rome and how in a way they were wasted on me, not because of the narcotics and pain, but because I was so limited about art, history, and things like that.

Edgar was quite smart about some things. He used to proofread at the press office, so he didn't read just his dirty magazines, which were mostly pictures anyway. He knew about other stuff, so I started to ask him about things I'd read in the paper. Then all of a sudden the paper stopped. "Edgar, where's my morning paper?" I asked him.

He smiled and said, "Sweetheart, we can't have you getting too smart, can we?"

This really bothered me, so I asked Dot's mother to bring me over her paper when she finished it. I'd read it and hide it under the mattress when I was through. I guess Edgar thought if I got too smart, I'd think hard about leaving him again. Then I asked her to start bringing me some of Dot's novels, and while Edgar was gone during the day I'd read. Dot told her mother to give me *Middlemarch*, but my favourite was *Wuthering Heights*. I cried when I read about Cathy dying and how Heathcliff suffered, even digging her up after she died. I thought of how Danny was somewhere down deep in the cold Atlantic, so I couldn't even dig him up and hold him. I really tried not to think of Danny as much now that I was expecting and Edgar had stopped hurting me. But I couldn't forget him. And I couldn't forget the way Edgar had been.

Edgar was very loving to me during those nine months, waiting on me and catering to me. I realized then that the only way he'd ever be really happy would be having me completely to himself. Then he could stop displaying me, torturing me, because that's what he did, and degrading me, which is what he also did. He could just enjoy me: to wash, shampoo, and polish—his very own little girl doll, forever in her bed, waiting for food and fondling. Not to be shared with anyone. Like the "Paper Doll" the Mills Brothers used to sing about.

14. The Pain Giver

I ASKED EDGAR, "Why do you suppose hurting me used to excite you?" And then, thinking about how he had blamed his mother at times for the way he was, I asked, "Was your Mommy mean to you?"

I remembered Margaret Clarke. She was a little dour woman with a tight disapproving mouth and dark hair pulled back in an ugly little knob. She didn't mix with the neighbours, and my only memory of her was listening to her call for Edgar and Shirley to come home for supper when they were very young. She and his father never seemed to go anywhere together, although on occasion she attended "the Kirk," the Presbyterian church, on her own.

Edgar got up from the bed where we'd been listening to the radio and lit a cigarette.

"You mean Maggie and her wooden spoon? Actually it was her hand from the beginning. She must have started as soon as I was born. I heard her once brag to a mother of one of Shirley's friends that I was 'clean' at twelve months. The woman looked at her and said, 'but he was only a baby. He was too young to be trained.' She answered, 'Even babies know about getting their bums warmed.'

"Mrs. Warren, who used to come to clean the house and the printing premises once a month, told me it was so bad she had to stop coming to our house. She just couldn't watch it. My mother would spank the hell out of me every hour on the hour for any stupid reason she could think of, from getting dirty to making a noise, even to falling down. She couldn't stand the old man, or men in general, and later on I figured she used to take it out on me. But when you're a kid, that's not how you think. You think that you're the worst little bastard in the world, and you must deserve it because you're the 'disgusting, filthy, little creature' your mother says you are.

"I can't remember when it didn't happen. Every day I'd get stripped down and she'd beat up on my bare ass with her tough little hand until I was hollerin' my head off, and like I said, anything and everything would bring it on. She didn't need an excuse, although she always pretended to have one." Edgar stood looking at me, pushed his thick straight hair away from his forehead, and gave me a humourless grin.

"I remember my first day of kindergarten. She was standing there. She never took my hand or kissed me or hugged me like I'd see other moms do with their kids. I figured I wasn't worthy, being such a dirty little creep. The teacher was Miss MacAlister, and Mom told her, 'I must warn you: Edgar's a very bad boy, and if he gives you any trouble you've only to say the word, and I'll warm his ass good and proper.'" Edgar's mimicking of his mother's voice was accurate—and weird.

"Remember Miss MacAlister? She looked like you, Angie—really pretty, with dark curly hair and big green eyes, and very tiny. She took my hand, and I could feel a current of love go right up my arm. She said, 'I don't anticipate any trouble with Edgar.'

"I fell in love with Miss MacAlister right then. Once she even put her arm around me and kissed me on the cheek. I almost passed out with joy. She said, 'You're a wonderful boy, Edgar, and smart too. Don't let anyone tell you you're not.' I always remembered her saying that." Edgar paused, and his voice became husky at the memory.

"It was the worst day of my life when my kindergarten

year was over and I had to leave her. I remember sitting in my seat trying not to cry—the last to leave. Then I saw the Spoon Lady standing by the classroom door. I knew I was going to get one of her thirty-minute specials for being the last to leave, but I didn't care." Edgar's flippant voice seemed strangely inconsistent with his words.

"I looked at Miss MacAlister. She was wiping her eyes, and she said to my mother, 'I'll really miss Edgar. He's been nothing but a pleasure.' Her reply was, 'It must be all the spankings he gets.' Christ, she was a real treasure.

"I was so hungry for love that one kind word from a teacher would catapult me into a year-long crush. In grade three, it was Miss Diamond, another little dark replica of you and Miss MacAlister. She once touched my arm to congratulate me on getting perfect in spelling. It was enough to trigger me off, and all I could think of was Miss Diamond coming into my room at night and kissing me and touching me all over.

"Remember, the Spoon Lady didn't miss a day with her bare-assed spankings, not a day, but when I was seven, I stopped hollering. It was like a little ritual. I'd come home, and I'd lose something or be late—anything would do—and she'd say 'you know the drill.' I'd go upstairs and up she'd come. I'd lie across her, her bony sharp knees diggin' into my chest while she'd whale away at my butt with her tough little hand."

When Edgar said, "You know the drill," he mimicked his mother's voice, and it chilled me. I had heard that voice before, at times when I hid in my crystal igloo, times I didn't want to remember.

"By the time I was twelve, I was used to it. That's not to say I looked forward to it, but it sure as hell didn't bother me like it used to. Lookin' back, it was beyond crazy. Here I was as tall as she was, with a wanger half the size it is now, and a little crown of feathers around the roots of my dick, and there she was whaling on me as if I were a two-year-old.

"She used to say, 'You're getting to be a big boy—it's time I used the wooden spoon. Better you start to behave and then it wouldn't happen at all.' But to her, it was like water to a man dying of thirst. After she was through—and she'd take about thirty minutes, maybe more—she'd have a flush on that little yellow face of hers, and she'd say, 'There, let that be a lesson to you.'"

Again, the memory of these words nudged me.

"Remember, it was the only way she'd ever touch me. She wouldn't even give me a bath after I was about three. She'd just fill the tub and toss a bar of soap at me and say, 'Clean yourself up.' If I didn't scour every inch it would be an excuse for one of her bare-assed lickings.

"Did she get off on it? Damn right. It was like heroin to her, and as I got older she was really hooked. Did I get off on it? Let's say a stinging whaling with a tough hand beat nothing at all, if it was the only way I was ever goin' to get touched. Sure, I was hooked on it. I had a history of twelve years of my mother whaling on my bare butt and never missing a day. A kid makes adjustments."

I did not return his tight smile. "It was in August," he continued, "the summer I turned twelve. Alec Woolridge and I were down off Waterford Bridge Road catching frogs because Alec had read somewhere that frog's legs were a delicacy and we were planning on selling them to a local restaurant. I got wet and dirty. When I arrived home, she said, 'Get upstairs, strip down, and wash yourself. You think I got nothin' better to do than wash dirty clothes for you. You know the drill.' I went upstairs and washed. I was a big kid by then, but she still figured she could whale on me with those tough little hands of hers.

"I still remember it. It was a hot day. We had those old yellow blinds, and there were flies crawling up them, but you could see the sun shining through. She sat down in her special chair. It was armless with a cushioned seat. She wanted comfort because at times she'd be there for a long time. She patted her sharp knobby knees and ordered me to lie across them and started slapping away. She slapped as hard as she could, and my ass was stinging and starting to heat up. She really had a good go at me that afternoon. She must have taken about forty minutes, give or take a little. Then she gave me a little slap, like a love pat, on my burning ass. It was the gentlest time she'd ever touched me.

"'You can get up now,' she said, and her voice was soft. I guess she was tired from all that exertion, and she was always better after a licking, like it somehow relieved her. I didn't move, and she gave me another little slap. 'Edgar, get up.' I still didn't move. The truth was I had a bone on, and I knew as soon as I got up it would be game over.

"'Up Edgar,' she yelled. I got up. She took one look at my erect dick and started to yell her head off, saying what a depraved little pervert I was and that all her 'discipline' was for nothing. She left the room. I started to get dressed, but I didn't have a chance. There she was with her wooden spoon beating me as hard as she could all over. She got me on the side of my right temple and split it open—look, you can still see this little white scar—and my arms and legs were bruised all to hell. When she was through, she told me to stay in my room as she couldn't bear the sight of me. I'd always been a disgusting little boy and this proved it.

"I would lie there watching the flies crawl up the yellow blinds. Shirley came up with a glass of water. Poor Shirley, she always felt sorry for me. In fact, she tried to tell my dad. But no one listened much to Shirley. She said, 'Did she hurt you bad, Gary?' She and the old man used to call me Gary instead of Edgar. I took a few gulps of the water, but then the downstairs bitch yelled out for Shirley to leave me alone. My head was pounding because she got me twice on the right temple and the top of the head with the full force of her stupid spoon." Edgar walked slowly over to the bed, took one of my cigarettes from the side table, and lit it before continuing. He smiled broadly at what I knew was my shocked face.

"I was big on sports then. I could skate better than any other kid in the class, and I was captain of the Junior Caribou softball team. That night my team had their first championship game, and I didn't want to miss it.

"The old man used to go to all my games. I really cared for him. He never laid a hand on me and used to call me 'son' when not 'Gary.' The trouble was he was always workin'. If he'd been around she'd never have gotten away with what she did, but lookin' back she was very sneaky about all her spankings, and only complained to him about how bad I was, which he always ignored anyway.

"You remember my old man? He was a big bull of a guy with a thick thatch of white hair and a barrel chest. I remember touching his hair in his coffin, and it was as thick as ever. He was only forty-two, and he was sick for two years. Remember, I dropped out in grade ten to help him? He was full of cancer they said—liver, lungs, bowels, the whole package—but he kept on workin' ... an' smokin' an' drinkin'. He said it was too late to give any of that up now.

"He left everything to me. He said he knew I'd take care of 'the old bitch' even if she didn't deserve it.

"Anyway, he came home at seven that night and right away asked for me 'cause he knew about the game. I heard that much from upstairs. I was really pissed that I was missing the game. The whole team was counting on me.

"He came upstairs. When he saw me, he said, 'Jesus Christ, who did that to you?' I said, 'She did.' He sat down, and I saw him run his hands through that thick thatch of hair of his. He was really upset.

"'How long she bin beatin' up on you?' I said, 'Every day for as long as I can remember. I can't remember her missin' a day. Sometimes I asked for it.'

"'Nope, you never asked for it,' he said. 'Not every day

you didn't. There's more to it than that. Her sister once told me her daddy diddled her and she hated men. I know she hated me. It was like sleepin' with frozen gristle. But I never thought she'd take it out on her own kid—such a good kid too, such a hard worker. How'd she do it?'

"'She tells me to strip down and lie across her knees. It lasts about half an hour a day—sometimes more, never less—until she's tired. She's got a tough hard hand, but I got used to it.'

"'Guess you had to. Yuh shudda told me, you know that.'

"'I used to think I deserved it. Later, I figured out she'd just look for reasons.'

"'No doubt in my mind. Crazy cunt—I'm sure she liked doin' it. You used to cry a lot when you were a little kid, and it used to bother me. I shudda protected you an' I didn't. Too busy workin' and avoiding her. I'll make it up to you. She'll never lay a hand on you again. You could make things really bad for her. All you have to do is show up in the state yer in at the softball game. They'd have the Children's Aid here in no time, and the sick bitch would never show her ugly little face at the Kirk again ... or you can just trust me.'

"He went downstairs, and I could hear him yelling at her—but you know something? She never did tell him about the erection. Perhaps she knew she caused it—all those whalings on my bare butt for all those years. I sort of missed them. They were, after all, the only contact I ever had with her. I guess that's why that last little pat on my burning ass triggered the hard-on. I would have settled for anything, but all I ever got was that tough little hand.

"She never laid a hand on me after that, but I never liked her. She never had a good word to say to me. I was glad to get her and Shirley out of the house, although I always felt sorry for poor Shirley—a really slow but kind little girl. I give the bitch money from the business every month, and she phones me, probably to be sure the money keeps coming in, but I got nothing to say to her, never did.

"After that I stopped sports. I used to help the ol' man every day after school and on weekends, partly to get away from her She'd say, 'Your father's office with his dirty magazines is the right place for you.'

"My dad had porn magazines. He'd bring them back when he'd been away on business trips and keep them in the press room. Later, I'd look at them and get off on the pictures. They were heavy stuff. He never had any at home, but she knew they were at the office. She really hated sex, but she sure as hell got herself off on whaling my bare ass.

"So now you know my dirty secrets, it's your turn. How about Hettie?"

"Mother was cold and critical, but there was nothing like that. That's awful."

"So next time I hurt you, you can think, poor Edgar, he's just getting his own back because of his bitch of a mother." He laughed when he said it, but it really troubled me. I kept thinking of the things he used to say during what I always thought of as my crystal chandelier period. They were exactly his mother's words, and his voice when he spoke was the same as hers would have been. Yet he didn't seem to make the connection.

"Since you seem to know what's behind what you do, perhaps you should talk to someone—like a doctor—and see if you can get help."

He just smiled and didn't answer.

15. The Intruder

I SAW ANOTHER SIDE to Edgar during the eleven-month wait. I saw he was capable of kindness, even love, and I saw that he could control himself if he wished. When my belly got big, he'd put his hands on it and try to feel the baby, and he'd rub my back and feet. If I hadn't known what he was capable of, I would have thought he was the most loving man in the world. But he'd hurt me so much, I couldn't forget it. I was still scared, still wary. I was always waiting, waiting for the pain. But it never came.

"Can you give her a Caesarean?" I heard him ask Dr. Macpherson when I went into labour. Dr. Macpherson asked him why, and he said, "It's safer, isn't it?' I knew that wasn't the reason he wanted it—he just didn't want any physical changes.

I had a normal birth. Bobby was a big baby, and I was in labour for several hours, but the joy I felt when I saw him made up for all the pain. I was so happy, for the first time in so long.

But then Edgar started to change back. What I'd been waiting eleven months for started again. It was as if I'd been given a reprieve, but now I had to pay for it, and he had to be rewarded for his good behaviour. I had never really trusted him, but now it was clear he'd just been manipulating me. And now there was the baby, an assurance that I couldn't leave.

A lot of Edgar's problem was his crazy jealousy, which

seemed to come from something even deeper. He was jealous of Danny and jealous of Dottie. And he was jealous of Bobby, jealous of every minute I'd spend with my little baby.

He'd come home for lunch and drain both breasts. "Please don't do this," I'd beg.

All the sex came back, rougher than ever, but again it was as if it were happening to someone else and that I was just looking on. I still cried out, but not enough. He always wanted feedback. "You're just dallying with me," he'd say.

I should never have had a baby. Edgar couldn't make room for anyone else.

Bobby was six months old, and I was still nursing him. He was fretful, not meeting his guidelines according to Dr. Spock's book—and I was starting to worry. Edgar was getting crazier and crazier. He always wanted my breasts available to him. I suspected it was because he was competing with Bobby. I hated it.

That evening I brought Edgar his dinner—steak, mashed potatoes, and peas. "I have to feed Bobby. He's been sleeping all afternoon and I'm full of milk."

"You don't have to do anything except strip and sit down in that chair so I can look at you while I'm eating."

"Can't this wait until later on tonight? I'll feel better once I nurse Bobby. He's really hungry."

"I don't give a fuck. It's time you learned who comes first in this house, and it's not some screaming little baby."

So I sat there. He kept munching away, looking at me. Then he pushed his plate away. Before I knew it, I was on the floor, but instead of holding my hips as he usually did, he held my breasts, one in each hand. He was squeezing them so hard I screamed. It made him climax.

"I'm taking Bobby and leaving you."

"I'll get the best lawyer in town and see the little bastard every weekend. How long do you think he'll survive with me having him every weekend?"

I felt myself go weak with fear.

The next day I made an appointment with Norman Marshall, who I'd been told was one of the few lawyers in St. John's who did family law. Divorce was not yet possible, but it was talked about, and associated with Confederation, which we all knew was coming.

I left Bobby with Mom and borrowed fifty dollars for my one-hour visit. Mom and I were speaking again because of our love for Bobby. I told her about Edgar's jealousy of the baby and found her sympathetic. I told her nothing else.

I paid my fifty dollars to the girl at reception, sat on one of the stout leather chairs, lit a cigarette, and waited. My throat had tightened, and my hands had become cold. Norman Marshall appeared in the reception area, smiling. He was about fifty, tall and ginger-haired, with a belly that showed he enjoyed his two-hour, roast beef, mid-day dinners. "We've met," he said, still smiling as he sat behind his desk, "at the Freemason's Ball. You probably don't remember. It was about two years ago, and I congratulated Edgar Clarke on his beautiful wife."

"You're a friend of my husband?"

"We're both Freemasons and belong to the Shriners, but he's not a close friend by any means. I've always liked him. Everyone likes Edgar."

How, I asked myself, could I tell this smiling pleasant man that the likeable Edgar Clarke had spent his happiest hours causing me pain?

"Is everything I tell you confidential?"

"Everything you tell me is privileged."

"Sometimes," I ventured, "people are different in private than in public. My life with Edgar has been ... difficult. He's a very jealous and possessive man."

"Is there any reason for this?" I didn't reply. Was Norman

Marshall hinting that perhaps I had somehow earned Edgar's jealousy? "We'll be proceeding in Family Court and I'll be showing you as a deserted wife and Edgar guilty of acts of violence, which would constitute 'danger to your life, limb, or health,' as the statute says. In other words, you'd be forced out of the house by his conduct, so it's best you move out before I serve him. There's some sophisticated terminology for all this, but I don't want to confuse you. Has there been physical violence?"

I hesitated. "I'd rather not say."

Norman Marshall shrugged, his smile gone. "Then I can hardly help you, can I?"

"You know Edgar and like him. I'm not interested in destroying his reputation and friendships. I just want to leave him and protect my son."

"The child's age?"

"Six months. What I want to know is: can I stop Edgar from seeing him if we separate? He has no use for the baby, and he may hurt him if I leave—to punish me."

Norman Marshall scowled. "Mothers are usually given custody of very young children, children of 'tender age' as the law says, and of older ones, except in rare cases of perceived harm or mental illness. But fathers have access unless there is an actual risk to the child. I think your husband will get access if he wants it, and the time will increase as the child gets older—unless you can prove there are risks to your son's safety."

"My baby may have some problems. Edgar calls Bobby names and resents my nursing if he wants my attention." I could not tell Norman he took Bobby's milk by nursing himself. It was all so humiliating. I could feel my heart beating, and I took a deep breath. I didn't trust Norman Marshall. I had met his wife Madeline Marshall at social gatherings, and she loved to gossip.

"Some fathers are irritated by crying babies. Has he

assaulted the child?"

"No. He's just told me if I leave, and he has access, the child won't survive."

"I'm sure he didn't mean that—not Edgar Clarke. He just wanted to be sure you wouldn't leave him." *So typical of men to protect each other.* I wanted to leave. But I was beginning to see the difficulties ahead.

"If, Mr. Marshall, I was to leave the island—just pick up and leave, and take the baby—what would happen?"

"Don't even think of it. Your husband might get a custody order in your absence if you remove the child from his permanent residence without his consent."

I got up. "Thank you for your time."

"Sorry not to be of more use to you. Many of us practising in this field just confine ourselves to domestic contracts or property matters. When it comes to property, women share only if they are on title or have made a direct contribution. But this doesn't seem to be your concern. There is no divorce here, as you know. Individual Canadian provinces have it, but they are waiting for a federal Divorce Act that would extend to Newfoundland if we join Canada. This new act might help you."

He paused and waited, but I sat silent, so he continued.

"As things are now, I'd have to apply to the Family Court, justify your leaving—based on your so-called 'desertion'— and attempt to show that your husband's conduct not only forced you to leave but could seriously impact on the well-being of your child. The conduct must show cruelty that consists of violence or injury, hopefully with a medical report to support it."

Again he stopped and waited, but I could not comment. I needed Dottie. So he continued.

"Few women from your class go to Family Court where most of those attending are self-represented. Many women would be reluctant to expose their private lives to legal and private scrutiny. Matters of custody and access would be ruled on at the time of the hearing."

Our eyes met, and then I looked away.

He knew I wasn't telling him everything, and I knew I couldn't. It would ruin Edgar, and everyone would know.

"If I were to give you a report from a doctor showing he … did things, would that help?" Norman Marshall stood up.

"Absolutely, provided it's relatively recent. If not, the courts might presume you condoned whatever happened. You have a six-month-old baby, so I would suggest that any cruelty should have occurred after the conception of the child. Hopefully, the court would take into consideration that you remained in an attempt to keep your marriage together. The doctrine of condonation should be interpreted flexibly in marital matters."

"Condonation?"

"Put up with it and forgive it. In other words, have sex." He smiled at me indulgently, as with a very young child. He walked slowly with me toward the door and continued. "I suggest if there is an episode of cruelty you confide the details and show evidence to a friend—better still visit your family doctor—although I warn you family doctors are often reluctant to be involved, especially if the husband is also his patient. We'll be bound by Canada's Divorce Act if Confederation ever comes, but for now we have our own act. You'll have a support claim for yourself and your son. Edgar's printing business is quite successful, I understand. He's a generous chap, a dependable contributor to the Shriners and Freemasons, so he'll probably agree to reasonable support."

"I don't want anything. I just want to leave."

"Rather short-sighted of you, Mrs. Clarke. It's been a relatively short marriage, but you do have some rights." He smiled at me indulgently again. He didn't understand, and it was my fault. I should have told Dot everything, and she should be here with me.

"My family's not poor, Mr. Marshall. My mother's family owns Bennett's Furs, and my father's an accountant. They'll help pay for your services." I noticed a change. He took my arm as we walked toward his office door, and even his voice became softer. It was obvious that other things could come before his fondness for Edgar.

"Of course, I know your father, and I've heard of your mother. I want you to consider what I've said and try to trust me. Sometimes these are ... delicate matters, but you must think of your wellbeing and that of your baby. This is a city of gossip, but people tire of things in time, and you may want to leave and start a life elsewhere. You're still very young. Write me a history of the marriage, and see your family doctor for a report. Come back to see me when you've done that, if you still want to leave. But don't do anything foolish like taking off with the child. I could get an *ex parte* restraining order if you fear your husband."

"*Ex parte?*"

"Behind his back, before he's served with papers." I could see the importance of Edgar's and Norman's friendship was evaporating fast.

It was raining outside and I wanted to smoke again, but I had to wait until I reached my parked car. I looked toward the Southside Hills, but they were invisible through the fog. The rain dropped like cold tears on my cheeks.

I went to pick up Bobby at Mom's. It was four o'clock. "Well?" She was holding Bobby, who was sleeping in her arms.

"He wants evidence of cruelty."

Her mouth tightened. She stood with Bobby, rocking him gently, and then traced her finger over his smooth, round cheek. She looked at me and sighed. "We must protect our baby. He must come first."

Rather than take Bobby and leave, I sat down and lit a cigarette. I had never had an intimate conversation with

Mom. In the years since Danny's death, I had felt and shown open hostility, but I felt a softening toward her at that moment. "Before I became pregnant and Bobby was born," I said softly, "Edgar could hurt me, but it was different. I sometimes felt ... numb. Once Bobby came, I became so much more vulnerable, so anxious to protect him. It's made me do things, things I'd never do before." Mom nodded, and we were both silent.

Then Mom said, "Finish your cigarette, Angela. You smoke too much."

I obeyed, and then I got up. Mom gently handed the sleeping Bobby over, but after she did so, she brushed back some of my rain-soaked hair. It was so strange. I felt my eyes burn. And then she rubbed my cheek with the back of her hand, in the same way that she'd traced her finger over Bobby's. We walked to the door together, neither of us speaking, and I knew that something had forever changed between us.

Edgar came home early, and dinner was not only not on the table, but not ready. And there was no dessert. Edgar loved dessert. I'd been thinking of emptying my sleeping capsules into his baked custard, and then getting a late-night flight to Florida with Bobby before I saw the lawyer.

"What did Norm Marshall tell you?" He was sipping his Crown Royal and smiling. My hand started to shake. "I have," he said, not losing his smile, "some great pictures for my lawyer. Might make them think you were going along with it all—just in case you've other ideas."

I thought of the photos he'd taken with his his new imported camera. Now he was using them to blackmail me. I didn't answer, but anger was choking me. I'd had eleven months of loving behaviour, and now this.

"Looked at your ass last night—it's a train wreck. You used to have a great, high, white little ass—a real turn-on. It's gone downhill since the hairbrush walloping, and I've had to keep you in line since the baby. You'd never get another guy with that ass. Course you're asking for it, just lyin' there like a piece of dead meat, not making a sound."

"If you don't like my ass, why don't you leave it alone." I spat it out.

"I didn't say I didn't like it. I'm just saying no other guy would. I still got some affection for it 'cause I did the damage."

"You're such a pig, Edgar." I said it as casually as I'd say *Do you want more dinner?* Usually this would bring about one of his spankings, followed by a filly ride, but he just kept his smile.

"I'm working on your tits. By the time I'm finished with them, they'll be worse than your ass. You got a lot of nursing ahead." He was planning to destroy my body so that no one else would ever want it. I wanted him dead. I felt the heaviness of hopelessness coming down, like after Danny.

Faint hiccups were coming from Bobby's bedroom. I moved from the table, but I felt Edgar's hand grip my wrist. "Forgetting? The first drink's always on me. You're gonna nurse this baby a lot longer than that one." He was unbuttoning my blouse. Edgar's nursing was as painful as everything else he did to me, and I shuddered. I could see this excited him. He loved this new way to give me pain. And I couldn't withdraw in my mind as I did with the spanking: it was too close, too intimate.

"You've taken your son's milk."

"They'll fill up again—you got a lot. You can share the wealth. Strip." I'd known it was coming: a hard ride around the track to teach the filly a lesson about seeing lawyers, not having food on the table, and not knowing who came first— and calling her husband a pig, even if he was one.

I would, I decided later, have to stop nursing Bobby or stop taking pain pills. Weaning him would be impossible with Edgar's growing demand for breast milk, even coming home at lunch for the privilege. I was worried about Bobby. He was just now holding up his head, and he was not attempting to sit up. The pediatrician had suggested testing at the Montreal Neurological Institute if things didn't improve. Perhaps it was the pain pills. But I didn't think so.

After Edgar had gone to bed, I sat smoking in the living room, finally wearing a dressing gown. He had not been concerned enough about the lawyer, perhaps knowing that I would be too ashamed to tell Norman everything. He knew me so well. Had Norman Marshall phoned him? I didn't think so. He was encouraging me to give him information and provide evidence. My bum had healed long ago, but it was permanently blue with some scarring, and it was always covered with bruises.

Going to court would be a nightmare, and Dottie had once told me that the cards were stacked against women. And there were the pictures. But I knew he'd not want to go to court. I could leave after, but his business was here. And everyone would know.

I went downstairs to the basement. Edgar's work table was piled with files filled with invoices and correspondence. There were no pictures. There were stacks of magazines. They were all alike: close-ups of women in bondage, anchored in chairs, waiting for torture or penetration—or both.

"You won't find them. They're at the office. I look at them at work when I'm bored, and I think of what I'll do when I get home." He was sitting on the basement steps. "The brat's crying."

I would see Dr. Macpherson, and I would get the report and some sleeping pills. I'd knock Edgar out at night, or perhaps permanently. I should have thought of it before, long before Bobby was born. I had changed. Perhaps it was Bobby, or the books Dottie had given me, but I knew I had value.

"Did you read it, Angie?" Dottie had asked, holding up my borrowed copy of *Middlemarch* when she'd visited me during my pregnancy. "She was a woman, but she wrote under the name George Eliot to find acceptance. She felt women had too much compassion. It held them back."

"Some have more compassion than others," I answered, smiling. I was happy to be pregnant. Edgar had stopped torturing me, and I was glad to see Dottie, so intense and so caring. I had missed her after the honeymoon, when Edgar had made my seeing her so difficult.

"I was reading about Anne Frank in the paper. She's a Jewish girl who hid in an attic in Holland, but the Nazis eventually hunted her down, and she died in a concentration camp from typhus. She was only fifteen, but she still believed in the basic goodness of people. I could never be as good as that. She kept a diary, and they might publish it."

I tried not to think too much about the war, as all thoughts seemed to lead to Danny. And as for basic goodness, Edgar had given me second thoughts about that.

Dottie sat down on the edge of the bed—slim and crisp, wearing her horned-rimmed glasses and dark suit—and took my hand in her cool slight one. "You seem so much better, Ducky, more like in the old days. You've even got a little pink in your cheeks." She'd looked down at my hand and spotted my painted nails. "Lord, luv, you've even got your nails painted pink."

I laughed. "It's Edgar, he does them."

She gave an unbelieving hoot. "I don't believe this. I've got to tell Wills. He'd never picture Edgar Clarke painting his wife's nails."

"He's been good since the pregnancy."

I noticed her looking at me intently, and when she spoke her voice had a sincere rasp. "And if he's never not, you'd tell me, wouldn't you? You know I'm always there for you."

But there were things I could never tell her.

16. Visiting Dr. Macpherson

D R. CAMPBELL MACPHERSON had been my doctor since he'd delivered me: a delivery that took place, as Hettie had informed both Daddy and me on several occasions, "after fifteen hours of unspeakable labour." He had not only completed the "unspeakable" delivery, but he had also seen me through chicken pox, measles, mumps, and bouts of flu. And he had supplied me with nerve pills when Danny was killed. He delivered Bobby. I loved Dr. Macpherson; he was like my grandfather, but a grandfather who had my medical history. I'd not taken Bobby to him for his six-month check-up, instead seeking out one of the new pediatricians. My reading of Dr. Spock had convinced me Bobby was not meeting his milestones. Now, seeing Dr. Macpherson, I regretted it. There was no one I could trust like him.

He sat behind his desk, his white hair dipping over his lined forehead, his sallow face falling in grey folds; but his blue eyes, looking at me under the drooping lids, were bright with affection. "How's my favourite patient? You look a little tired—the baby keeping you up?"

"I need some more sleeping pills and pain pills."

"Nembutal and Empirin codeine." He scrawled on his pad, signed it, tore off a sheet, and handed it to me. "You seem to need a lot of pain pills. Not good to take too many of those, with you nursing that baby. Most of my patients bottle-feed, but I knew you'd be different. I was impressed but not surprised: I knew you'd do the right thing." I wanted to cry. I felt like a girl who'd done very much the wrong thing. "Everything healed up and back to normal?"

"I spot all the time—it never stops."

"You've resumed sexual activity?"

"It started again when the baby was a week old, and it's never stopped. It's every night, and he's very rough." Dr. Macpherson's smile was gone.

"Let's examine you." In spite of his gentle gloved hand, I was obviously hurting, and I saw him lift his eyebrows at my lack of pubic hair. "You're very sensitive. What's this man done to you? Your genitals are ravaged."

"So is my bum." I turned on the examining table, and he passed his smooth gloved hands over my bum cheeks.

"They're full of bruises, and seem discoloured," he murmured.

I told him everything. When I stopped, I was crying. When I looked at Dr. Macpherson, his head was turned and tears were running down his lined cheeks. "Angela, where'd you get a sick monster like this? A sweet, sensitive, joyful, young woman tortured by a man who'd be in competition with the Marquis de Sade. Sex should wait for three months after the birth, some say longer, and I told Clarke that after the delivery. I said it humorously, but he got the message. I always tell the husbands the same thing. He wanted me to perform a Caesarean. I thought it strange since there was no need for it. And you'd already had repairs in Montreal. You should let me tell your mother. Hettie would take him on. You know what you have to do …"

"I've seen Norman Marshall, and he said to get a medical report for court. He warned me Edgar could get access to Bobby. He's jealous of the baby, and he can't have access."

"I'll give you a report, and I'll go to court—you know I'll do that. In the meantime, I'm very concerned, Angela. I fear he's too much for you, this mentally ill man." Dr. Macpherson looked old.

"I'm stronger than I was."

"Keep him away from you. You shouldn't still be bleeding. And tell him you've seen me, and that I'll see him in court." He sighed. "I'm no spring chicken, Angela, and I've got a few health issues of my own. Don't delay too long, my dear. You've got your prescriptions. You're not considering taking too many of those Nembutals, I hope. Better things are in store."

"No, I won't do that. I couldn't leave Bobby with him."

"You should tell Hettie."

"I tried to escape once, and she told him."

"Did she know what he'd been up to?"

"No."

"You should have told her." Dr. Macpherson sighed as I got up to leave. I knew I'd shocked and worried him, but I was glad I'd have his support. "Don't delay any of this. And no sex. Keep him away from you."

I thought of Dr. Grotteria and how I should have listened. But I was weaker then.

Large white flakes were falling and while the days were getting longer, it was still dark at suppertime. From a distance I could smell the harsh saltwater of the harbour, and the cold air made my cheeks tingle. I walked, head down, through the cold and snow to my parked car, where snow was already starting to pile up on the windshield. I got into the chilled car and lit a cigarette. Through the curtain of slowly falling flakes, I saw Danny on the sidewalk. He was strolling toward me. He had that jaunty little walk of his. No one else walked like that, and he wore a white sailor suit—the same one he'd worn when I'd seen him in Italy—and his white sailor's cap was perched on one side. He was smiling, the way he always did when he saw me. I got out of the car and ran toward him. Then he was gone, and there was only the streetlight, surrounded by flies of snow, and I was standing there alone, while all around me curtains of snow were dropping down.

I walked back to the car, empty with loss. It was late, and Edgar wouldn't be happy. I should have made an earlier appointment with the doctor. I drove up Duckworth Street, worried about time, but with a sense of comfort from seeing Danny and having Dr. Macpherson's support. The wipers clicked back and forth, and a solid ridge of snow was building up at the sides of the windshield. I shuddered and turned on the heat. My breasts were filling up, pressing painfully against my bra. I would try to stop him until we could settle things. He was capable of better. He could control himself. I had not predicted his jealousy of our baby—yet another example of my stupidity. He had been jealous of everything else in my life. I parked the car and went into Edward's Pharmacy.

I stopped at my mom's to pick up Bobby. "What did Dr. Cam say?" asked Mom, with a small curved smile. She always referred to Dr. Macpherson affectionately as Dr. Cam, except when she spoke of his "cruelty" in allowing her fifteen hours of unrelieved labour.

"He's concerned about my spotting, and he'll give me a medical report."

She waited for me to tell her what I never had.

I couldn't.

Bobby was crying. I would attempt solids soon—Dr. Spock had recommended them. I decided to nurse him at Mom's. I wasn't ready to go home.

I looked out the window. The lights over the door and inside the house were on, and Edgar's car was in the driveway.

"I've nothing ready for dinner."

"Surely he'll understand. You really cater to him, Angela. You're not his servant. The Clarkes had no social position in this town until Edgar was so successful with the printing business."

When I got home, Edgar was in the front room drinking. He was furious. I placed Bobby in his crib upstairs, came down, and sat opposite him. "We have to talk. Can I get you some scrambled eggs first?"

"I want my fucking dinner. You think you can treat me like dirt, like nothing, coming home late and leaving the brat with your mother for the afternoon. Who you been meeting?"

"I'll get you something to eat."

"I don't want fucking food. Where the hell were you?"

"I saw Dr. Macpherson. He examined me, and I told him everything. He's giving me a report for Norman Marshall, and he'll come to court. He said you'd ravaged my genitals—that should make you happy—and that you had no right forcing sex a week after Bobby came. He'd told you to wait three months, but, of course, you didn't care."

"You forget I waited for eleven months so you could produce the retard. I never had any appreciation for that from you. That old bastard probably got off looking at your shaved twat and everything else."

"Dr. Macpherson delivered me, Edgar. He was so upset by what you'd done to me, he cried."

Edgar just sat there looking at me. It was obvious that he'd never thought I'd go so far, taking for granted that my shame would prevent it. Now I'd exposed him to Dr. Macpherson, one of St. John's most respected doctors, who was going to support me in a court action.

He stayed in the chair, periodically getting up to fill his glass, getting drunk. He cursed under his breath. And he left me alone.

It was all I'd ever wanted from him.

The next morning, I telephoned Dot, who was in Halifax, hoping she'd not be in class. I told her I'd seen Norman

Marshall and Dr. Macpherson, and told her I was going to court. There was silence. And then she said, "What will the medical report say?"

"Things I didn't want to tell you. Things he's done. Things I didn't want to worry you about." I heard her give a sharp intake of air, and when she spoke her voice was a mixture of anger and concern.

"And you didn't trust me enough to tell me."

"I trust you. That wasn't it. It was very hard for me to talk about some of the things. When it's all over, I'll tell you more." There was silence again. When Dot spoke her voice was almost harsh.

"Promise me, Angie, you won't back down on this. It's an insult to our friendship that you wouldn't tell me more before. You seem to be forgetting ... so much." I started to cry, and her voice softened. "At least you're doing it now. What a weird character that Edgar is, going from painting your nails to abuse—at least I suspect it's abuse."

I didn't answer.

"I'll see you at Easter," she continued. "I wish I was there. Promise me you won't back down."

I promised.

I picked up the medical report a week later from Dr. Macpherson's office and read it parked in Mom's driveway. It was a two-page report giving all my medical history and describing in specific detail the damage done to me.

My cheeks burned as I read it. I cringed at the thought of Norman Marshall knowing the details of what Edgar had done to me. And I was ashamed of myself for letting it happen. His legal secretary would read it, as would Edgar's lawyer and the judge. Worse, Edgar would pretend I'd encouraged it; he would show everyone those vulgar pictures he'd taken.

They'd never believe him, not with Dr. Macpherson as my witness. They'd know that no one in their right mind would have ever allowed the damage he'd done. But had I been in my right mind? Did I think I deserved it all for marrying him in the first place?

The last paragraph of the report said: *In view of the widespread damage done to this young woman by her husband, it is my opinion that he suffers from a sadistic sexual disorder bordering on mental illness, which may or may not be treatable. An individual with these propensities could pose a threat to a child, even if his motivation were merely to cause distress to the wife, rather than injury to the child himself. I would ask this court to consider my recommendation, which is that Edgar Clarke be restrained from having contact with either his wife or son until long-term therapy dictates otherwise. I am willing to attend court to substantiate all aspects of this report.*

I went into my childhood home, headed for the bookcase, and placed the report in *Middlemarch*. When I turned, Mom was watching me, holding Bobby in her arms. He gave me a little smile. Such a pretty baby. I kissed his round warm cheek when I took him from her arms.

17. Nembutal and Baked Custard

EDGAR DID NOT COME near me for two weeks. He'd come home, eat his dinner without speaking, and then go upstairs and lie on his bed, smoking and drinking and listening to the radio. I'd been sleeping on a pull-out in Bobby's room. We'd gone to the Shriners ball at Edgar's insistence, but he'd hardly spoken to me, merely commenting after I'd danced with one of his friends, "If he saw your ass he wouldn't want to go near you."

Mom wouldn't look at or speak to him.

"You been spilling your guts to Hettie?"

"Never."

There were two explanations for her behaviour: she'd spoken to Dr. Cam or she'd read his report.

I phoned Norman Marshall, telling him I'd received the medical report. "Bring it in," he said, "and then write a history of your marriage and complete a financial statement. We'll proceed on violence, and we'll go on desertion caused by his violence, and have him served with papers before June. With any luck we'll make the fall list and get it heard before the end of the fall sittings. It'll get a lot of publicity—so few trials from your kind of people." He was enthusiastic.

I wasn't. The thought of having my private life with Edgar exposed to others made me go weak inside. It was the hurtful, intimate things he'd done, the things that were in Dr. Cam's report, that I couldn't stand people knowing about.

I wouldn't be able to face anyone ever again, and Mom would be so embarrassed and humiliated, especially when she'd always considered herself so superior to everyone else. I thought of myself standing in a witness box describing certain happenings, and I felt myself break out in a full body flush. I'd probably vomit, right there in the courtroom. They'd ask, *"What's her problem, letting him do that?"* I asked myself the same question.

That night I went upstairs and sat on the edge of the bed where Edgar was lying, listening to the radio. "Norman wants me to bring in the medical report and a marriage history. Edgar, he said there'd be a lot of publicity—so few family law cases here. Do you really want this? It'll be awful for us both, everyone hearing about the details of our wretched marriage. Why not agree to signing a separation agreement? Most people do that. Give me custody of Bobby, and we'll get a divorce when it becomes legal. You don't want to see Bobby—it's just to torment me, you know that. I don't want anything from you. Nothing. Norman is mad about that. Just for once, let's do something right. The marriage is dead; it should never have happened. Now let's end it." I was short of breath, and I felt my heart beating when I'd finished. I was trying to appeal to a sensible Edgar Clarke, a rational man, a man who I'd never seen surface when it came to our marriage. Looking back, even those eleven months weren't normal, just a temporary break where I became Edgar's very own paper doll.

"You chickening out? You'd never make it inside a courtroom." He thought being sensible was being weak, and he was counting on my being weak.

After that, I started writing a history of the marriage, and it troubled me. It forced me to see what had happened apart from the pain. I saw it from a distance. I'd been so flimsy, always giving in, never thinking I had any value. The history was not only of Edgar's cruelty, but of me as his victim. At times, even his accomplice. No wonder he was counting on me to give in. I always had.

I phoned Dr. Macpherson's office a week later. I was still spotting, and I wanted him to see Bobby. I didn't like what the pediatrician had told me, and I wanted his opinion. The receptionist answered the phone. "Dr. Macpherson is no longer carrying on a practice. His replacement, Dr. Abbott, would be happy to see you."

The obituary took up a half page in *The Daily News*: *Well Loved Local Doctor, Campbell Langdon Macpherson, Dead at 78*. I cried throughout the funeral service, and then I picked up Bobby from Mom.

"It's good you got that report," she said. Then I knew why she wasn't speaking to Edgar.

When I phoned Norman Marshall, he was very curt. I'd not only delayed coming in with my history but, as he said, "Now you can't use your report, which I've never seen." According to Norman, Dr. Macpherson had to be available as a witness and then for cross-examination, or the report would not be "admissible." I was to produce a report from another doctor. "Take a serious interest in your own case," he added.

Edgar was ecstatic. He had given my body an undeserved holiday, and now it started all over again. This time I fought back, but it seemed to excite him even more.

Bobby's round head is clustered with wisps of soft brown curls and when he nurses fine tendrils cling to his moist forehead. I see his cheeks are smooth and full and his eyes, like mine, are clear green with long black lashes, curling against his cheeks when he sleeps. When he's awake, I draw my finger along his curved cheek, and he smiles. But his eyes will not focus. They slide past me and focus on the air, as if the air were smiling. I take his slight cool hands, like small white wings that wave in the air, and pull him up gently to strengthen his back. Then I slowly release him, back down to the soft mattress. This is what the book tells me to do. Bobby owns all my mornings.

I was going to stop nursing Bobby because each night, and at lunch, Edgar insisted on nursing first, and by the time he was through my milk was gone and more sucking was painful. It was as if the death of Dr. Macpherson had set him free. I was sure he was getting advice from his lawyer, who he refused to name.

It was Monday, during the first week of April. The night before, Edgar had gone back to his old ways, and he'd refused to let me go to Bobby, who was crying. When he'd finished with me, I felt myself sliding into my old feeling of hopelessness, and it was only Bobby's need for me that kept me going. I would, I decided, see Dr. Abbott the following week. He could see all the fresh bruises and produce a new report. I'd not sacrifice my little baby to Edgar's mad jealousy.

I made baked custard, and then I carefully pulled apart three capsules, mixed the powdered contents through the custard in Edgar's Pyrex dish, and covered it with tinned peaches and maple syrup. Edgar ate it all.

At eight o'clock he was snoring in his chair, and when I woke him up for bed, he was groggy and barely made it up the stairs.

I used four capsules each night, just to be sure. Edgar loved his desserts, and their sweetness would disguise any of the capsules' taste.

The next night we had chocolate mousse, Edgar's favourite. I used melted chocolate, and covered the whole dish with whipped cream, its taste enhanced with sugar and vanilla. When I went to nurse Bobby, Edgar rose, but sank back in his chair. "I'm fucking exhausted," he growled. "You may be rid of me sooner than you think."

On Wednesday night, we had apple crisp with ice cream, another of Edgar's favourites. I doctored the ice cream and then poured butterscotch sauce over it. He talked to me as he shovelled it down. "Saw Parsons today. He took some blood and urine samples. He thinks I might have blood cancer, with my bein' dead tired every night."

Dr. Parsons had seen Edgar's father through stomach cancer, and Edgar liked him. He had called him "a young guy who was up on all the latest stuff."

Would the Nembutal show up in the blood tests? I hid my Nembutal phial in my boots in the hall closet.

On Thursday, Edgar came home early. He was quiet. He scowled when Bobby started fussing from a blanket I'd placed on the floor to encourage movement, and he scowled again when I picked the baby up and sat with him in my arms. "You got him ruined."

I served Edgar pork chops and Nembutal-free pancakes with syrup for dessert.

"Put down Dumbo, and come over here." The nickname cut through me like a knife. I placed Bobby back on his blanket, and sat down at the table. "I want you to eat these pancakes."

"I'm really not hungry."

"Eat."

I ate the pancakes and gave him a weak smile.

"You've been trying to kill me."

"You're out of your mind."

"Parsons said my blood's got traces of pentobarbital, the same drug they use on death-row killers. You've been giving it to me in my food. I'm waiting for you to keel over from those pancakes."

"I won't keel over."

"I'm gonna check with Edward's. Where you keep your pills?"

"I only have pain pills." But he was on the phone to the drugstore. My heart was thudding and my throat closing.

"Edgar Clarke. You filled a prescription for sleeping pills for my wife. She says they're knocking her out, and I was wondering what's in 'em." There was a pause. "Brand name Nembutal, main ingredient pentobarbital. Strong, eh?" There was another pause. "Appreciate the information." He turned to me. "How many you been givin' me, cunt?" I knew Edgar wanted to throttle me, but he was not a giver of black eyes and broken bones. "If you don't tell me," he said softly, "I'll phone the constabulary and have you charged with attempted murder. Then I guess I'll have to take care of Dumbo."

"I wasn't trying to kill you, Edgar," I said, my voice high with panic. "I was trying to make you tired for a few days so you'd give my body a break. You've got me spotting again, and you're taking Bobby's milk. If I'd wanted to kill you, I'd have given you more than four capsules a night."

"Get the bottle." I got up and went to the hall closet. I was shaking. I wished I'd killed him. Edgar shook out the capsules and counted them. "Eleven gone. Looks like you cut them down to three one night. I'll keep these; you won't need them again." He sat back and smiled. "I'll let you keep your pain pills. This will put an end to your legal nonsense, once and for all. I phoned my lawyer after I saw Parsons—he's way ahead of Marshall. He said they'd never give custody to a woman who tried to murder her husband. God knows what she'd do to a backward child. And the bloodwork is evidence."

I saw my life stretching ahead of me, a grey foggy path. And I couldn't end it—I couldn't leave Bobby with him.

He knew I wasn't trying to kill him.

"From now on," he said, his voice disarming and soft, "you will start serving dinner as you did before. There'll be no more nonsense about the nursing. Your breasts are mine. I'll be checking on you, and when you leave the house, you'll phone me first. You're a tricky and devious little bitch, and I've obviously got to keep you in line." All excuses for the torment to come.

The next week I stopped nursing Bobby and renewed my pain pills.

18. Creating a Precedent

In September 1946, Wills and I were admitted to Dalhousie law school. I was the only woman in a class of fifty men. "I want you to remember, gentlemen, that there is now a lady in our midst. I would caution you to watch your language at all times." Professor Dryden had authored the well-respected Dryden on Contracts, which he had taught at the university for fifteen years. There were general snickers around the class, and I felt my face burn. Next to me Wills was shaking in his seat with barely contained laughter.

"Arsehole," I hissed and kicked him as hard as I could on his good leg.

"She's a Newfoundlander," croaked a voice from the back.

"Am I to surmise that this disentitles her to the label of 'lady'?" scolded Dryden. "And am I to conclude that Newfoundland women tolerate swearing?" This produced another even louder snicker from my male colleagues.

They called me Lady Campbell for the next two months, then Lady, and finally Campbell Two. Wills was Campbell One. He was really popular. I led the class in contracts, which should have sent a message to everyone, including Professor Dryden, and certainly Wills, who ended up with a B minus.

We went home for Christmas in time to see Angie's new baby boy, a beautiful child with Angie's face. Edgar for once was pleasant and civil to us when we attended the reception following the christening.

"I hope," I whispered to Angie, "the empty pocket is filled."

I went home in June 1947 to work in Pop's law office for the summer. Wills was doing a two-month stint with the Justice Department. In the summer of 1947, politics, the island's favourite blood sport continued to heat up, as it had since the establishing of a National Convention the previous year. The choices of the future electorate were an independent island, called Responsible Government; a continuation of Commission of Government, which neither the British or the Newfoundlanders wanted; or even an economic union with the United States. The island's love affair with the Americans—or Yanks—was ongoing, as not only had their bases provided employment, but they had married thousands of local girls. But another option was surfacing.

Joey Smallwood—five-foot-four and one hundred and thirty pounds, complete with bowtie and owl-like glasses; a failed businessman but successful journalist and spellbinding speaker—was everywhere. His radio show, known as The Barrelman, had reached all corners of the island, an island he was now bombarding with ceaseless propaganda on the benefits of Confederation and the necessity of adding it as an alternative to the National Convention's choices. In some ways, he was right. Poverty would be eradicated—but at a price. The islanders were reluctant to lose their unique identity.

"If they gave you an enema, they'd bury you in a shoebox," croaked one phone-in listener to Joey on his radio show, sick to death of listening to him. The comment sent Pop into paroxysms of laughter when he repeated it at dinner.

I visited Angie during lunch hours, at times when she told me Edgar was not coming home, and even briefly in the mornings, when I noticed Edgar had left for work. I did not want to visit when he was home. Angie was always so nervous, and I saw that he was always hovering, listening to our conversation so I had to be careful what I said. I knew he resented my visits. In the mornings, I watched as Angie poured our tea, noting her fragile, pale hands as she held the china teapot and the mauve smudges under her eyes. I ached with concern for her.

I saw Angie, the perfect mother, with a son, Robert Edgar, who was perhaps not as perfect. "He's only now rolling over and sitting up, and he's nine months old. I've seen a physiotherapist and read books to help me learn how to strengthen his muscles." Her devotion was endless: focused and all-consuming. Edgar, on the other hand, had gone back to his usual scowling self.

"We won't be held responsible for this," Hettie hissed to me. "Edgar has two cousins severely retarded, and his sister's strange and had to go to a special school. If I'd known, I'd have stopped the marriage. I could have, you know. Angie was never that anxious to marry; she just sort of went along with it because he kept pressuring her. He refers to little Bobby as Dud or Dumbo—a horrible man. Poor Angela. And she stayed in bed for nine months to have the child." Hettie was on the right side for once. I watched her with this still, beautiful child, finally sitting up, and always with a smile. She played with him, using soft toys to hide and then pop up and tracing little circles in his palm. She tickled his arms with her fingers, which then ran up like mice and settled under his arm. She'd do anything to encourage a little animation. For the first time, I liked her. And it was sad: her only grandchild. There would be no more. The Montreal neurologist and a geneticist had cautioned Angie that similar problems could happen with any future children—not that Angie could carry another.

"Mom's so good with Bobby," said Angie. "She's read up on treatment for slow children, and she's so devoted." I noted the word slow rather than retarded or handicapped, which Bobby assuredly was. I thought of how Edgar calling the child Dud and Dumbo must hurt her.

"Look at him! He's trying to crawl," Angie lilted one afternoon. "He's such a good boy." It was after five o'clock in

August, and I was back from Pop's office. I thought I'd drop in, hoping Edgar would be late from his printing shop, but in he came, scowling as usual.

"Have we been so busy with Dumbo that we haven't made dinner?"

A shadow passed over Angie's face. Conscious of my presence, she said brightly, "Not to worry, there's a casserole in the oven."

"She's making the Dud into a little suck," he complained. "If he was normal, he'd be a genius by now." He averted his eyes from Bobby and told Angie he'd be taking his dinner in the dining room.

"I have to leave," I said. "I have to help Ma with dinner. It's unfair to have her serve two extra every night."

"You don't have to go," Angie pleaded. "Let me get you a drink. Edgar always has lots of booze around." She lit a cigarette and I noticed a slight tremor in her hand.

"I really can't, luv," I said. "Bobby's really making progress, and it's all due to your efforts." I kissed her. She smelled of cigarettes and sadness.

"And Mom's," she said.

"He even resents that sweet little boy," I later stormed at the dinner table. "He calls him ugly names and resents the fact that Angie's devoting her life to helping him."

"She should have left him after the honeymoon. That should have been enough," Wills growled. I saw Ma's face and knew she was bursting to know what had happened on the honeymoon.

"I never liked him, Dottie. He was always such an odd duck. The way he used to watch little Angie ..."

"Now that it looks like we might be joining Canada, she can get a divorce someday," said Pop. "We'll all be dumping our old harps after Confederation—won't we, Lil?" Ma merely gave him a blank look, as if being compared to an aged female seal were an everyday occurrence.

"I was thinking of dumping Dot," added Wills. "Can't have a wife getting better marks than her husband in her law exams; it's crushing to the male ego."

Everyone hooted. Pop was very proud of me. If you had to have a daughter, at least you could take pride in the fact that she was smart enough to become a lawyer and to marry a guy you could have a few laughs with.

Before I left for second year I went over to say goodbye. The early fall sun poured through the windows of Angie's living room and illuminated the face of Bobby, who was now crawling on the thick floor rug. Angie was wearing a sleeveless blouse, and I could see that her arms were white and thin. I rubbed her upper arm and felt its coolness through my fingertips. I felt a sense of sadness, an urge to protect her, and a sense of frustration at what I feared to be my own lack of action. "You were going to leave," I whispered, although we were alone. "You even saw a lawyer. You weren't going to back down—you promised. And I wanted to help. Now you never mention it."

"Dr. Cam died, and other things happened. I still want to leave, but now it's more difficult. Perhaps when you become a lawyer you can help."

I said, "Oh Angie," and placed my arms around her. It was like embracing a statue. I felt she was frozen in some sort of time warp, where she remained remote. Then I felt her sobbing against me, and I felt the same futility I'd felt after her honeymoon. "You must," I said, no longer whispering, "let me help. I know things are going on, bad things, things you don't want to share. But I can't help unless you let me."

She didn't answer. She only looked at me with tear-filled eyes, and said softly, "I'll miss you, Dottie."

19. Edgar

IT WAS CHRISTMAS OF 1947, and Bobby was starting to walk now, but only for a few seconds before he fell over. Angie would kneel on the floor and coo, "Come to Mama, Sweetie, come to Mama." Most sixteen-month-olds were walking around and climbing on the furniture, but Bobby was trying, with a great deal of encouragement. He smiled a lot, even when he fell, which was often. Such a pretty little guy, with Angie's curls, her big green eyes, and his own turned-up nose.

Edgar had taken the week between Christmas and New Year's off. Angie confided that he was drinking a lot and complaining of a recent decline in the printing business. On Wednesday of that week, he was returning to his press room to complete an unexpected order. "I really want to see you," Angie told me. "You're leaving in ten days, and I miss you like mad. I want to talk to you about something."

It was a cold but sunny day. Icicles, like daggers, were dripping from the eaves of the roofs, and waves of snow were scattered with embedded crystals. Wills had shovelled our path so that I could trot across to Angie's in my new boots, a Christmas gift from Ma. "Can't let Pop get a heart attack," he murmured to me. I thought of his own dad, dead at fifty-seven, and how much I loved my big, smiling Wills.

"Don't know where I got you," I cooed, puckering up for a kiss on the way out.

"It was your loose, lurid, and promiscuous lifestyle," he drawled. "A form of entrapment."

I was still smiling when I reached Angie's, where the path had not been shovelled. She was waiting for me. She had a glass of rye and ginger in one hand, which she handed to me, and a cigarette steaming in the other. "You'll need more than a cup of tea when you hear what I've got to tell you."

Bobby, dressed in corduroy pants and a hand-knit cardigan, was in the living room, toddling around as clumsy as ever, holding on to the chairs and coffee table. "Come over sweetheart. Come over and show Auntie Dottie what Grannie Bennett knit for you for Christmas."

He was approaching me tentatively, a little smile on his face. If you didn't know, you'd never suspect how severely limited he was. He was so immaculately and beautifully kept.

It was then that the door opened, and Edgar stood bulked against the doorway. It was obvious he'd been drinking—his unshaven face carried an unaccustomed flush and his eyes were shot with red.

The child dropped to his knees, any smile erased, and scampered more than crawled toward a large leather chair and hid behind it. I heard a noise, somewhere between a whine and a whimper.

"Come outta there, Dud," Edgar rasped. "Your mommy's made you such a suck that you can't even say hello to your ol' man."

"You scare him," spat Angie. "You're way too rough with him, barking out orders he doesn't understand."

"Who'da thought it, Dot, that I'd end up like this, with a dud kid who's a retard and a wife who cares about nothin' else.'Course she used to care about her railroad boy, really cared about him, but now she's got little Dumbo here to take his place. To think I used to spend hours watching her door so I wouldn't miss a glimpse of her when she left the house."

Behind the chair the whimpering increased. "If you don't stop snivellin', I'll really give you something to cry about."

"Why don't you leave? Dot doesn't want to hear your drunken ravings." Angie went and picked up Bobby, whose whimpering had now increased to loud sobs.

"I have to go," I said.

"No. Stay. I want you to hear this. Did you know that Hettie Bennett used to think you and Angie had an 'unnatural relationship?' 'Course she didn't know about all the screwing her daughter did with the railroad boy on the graves of the General Protestant Cemetery. Did she tell you she brought all his letters on our honeymoon and I had to bang him out of her?

"I had a few drinks at the bar but I thought she still hadn't had enough, so when I got back I cracked her little ass open. I carved it up so good she needed twenty stitches. We couldn't even see Venice. But she'd brought it on herself—she knew that."

I sat, transfixed, averting my eyes from Angie, who sat mute, holding the child. My mouth felt parched, and when I spoke my voice broke. "Why are you telling me this?"

"She behaved after that 'cause I never missed a night pounding the crap out of her, and beating up on her little ass.

She got her punishments, but it wasn't enough." He pulled up a chair and lit a cigarette, his voice husky with shared confidences.

"Perhaps you should be arrested," I blurted out, "and locked up forever, like an animal in a cage."

For the first time, a smile crossed his face. My anger gratified him; it gave him the impetus to continue.

He went on, describing the August pre-wedding assault in great detail—details that Angie had never told me. But I remembered the way she'd been at my wedding.

I got up, nauseated with anger and hatred. "Do you realize

what you're telling me? You could be charged with assault under the *Criminal Code*. Of course brutality and law-breaking mean nothing to a psychopath like yourself." I could see he was pleased. This was what he wanted, for me to share in Angie's torture.

"I carried her into the bedroom. She wasn't making a sound. I said, 'Are you ready for what you're goin' to get?' She was used to that by now. She just looked at me and said, 'Don't do it, Edgar.' Then those big green eyes of hers rolled back and she passed out."

A gush of horror transfused me. I was chilled and revolted by him, but also furious with her. Why had she permitted this? And why hadn't she told me?

"I'm leaving, Edgar," I told him. "I've heard enough. And Angie, it's still not too late for you. You've married a madman, but you don't have to stay in the asylum. Edgar, you're a sadistic lunatic." He did not refute this. I stood with my hand on the doorknob, but he was driven to continue.

"You know what? I thought I'd killed her. Really did. Guess it was the pain. I didn't hold back, and she couldn't take it. When she finally woke up she said she was going to leave. I knew I'd gone too far. I got jealous, the same as on the ship, but this time it shouldn't have fired me up that much. Trouble with me is once I start it takes over, really does.

"You may have seen how she was at your wedding. Her butt was a mess. The breaks and welts went away, but the colour changed for good; it stayed blue, the colour of veins. She said to me, 'you've ruined my bum.' I told her that no one else was ever going to see it but me.

"I mostly just used my hand after that. She told me once it was the most pain she'd ever had—I guess that's why she fainted. She said that having the baby was nothing compared to that whaling and some of the rough sex I'd given her. She told me that the night she said she was leaving. I admit I was way out of line with that hairbrush shellacking."

My hand was frozen to the doorknob. My crawling revulsion kept me there, a captive audience to a drama too horrendous to contemplate. Bobby was asleep, and I saw Angie gently place him on the sofa. I knew she wanted me to leave.

When I spoke my voice was harsh and strained. "Any more admissions, Edgar? There should be dozens more. You may regret telling me all this." He ignored me but continued as if lost in his own reverie.

"She had that little girl quality. She always had that. Not childish, but childlike. That's why I cared for her; that's why she turned me on. She always knew what I was thinking, and she was a little shy. It sounds crazy, but she was—that's why I got away with so much. She never wanted anyone to know what I used to do to her."

Angie started to get up, her face a mixture of frustration and embarrassment, but then he was behind her, placing two large paws on her slight shoulders. She shuddered, and he continued, his voice disarmingly soft, almost reverential, telling me things, intimate things, things she'd never want me to know.

"Dr. Macpherson said in his report that I'd ravaged her genitals. It takes a lot of work and a lot of screaming to ravage a woman's genitals—doesn't it, Angie?" I glanced at Angie. She was sitting there watching me, her face maroon, tears of humiliation rolling down her cheeks. "She tried to get my mind on something else. It was cute. Like I said, Angie's a little girl. She said, 'Edgar, would you like me to service you?' For a moment I could feel my throat get tight—that's how jealous I always get—and I said, 'Where did you learn how to service a man?' She said, 'I don't know how, but you can teach me. I'll do everything you tell me.' I said, 'I don't think you'd be that good at it. Anyway, I'm not into it.'"

I opened the front door, and a cold draft of air came in, welcoming in its freshness. Edgar continued, ignoring the fact I was leaving. "I know you think I'm a brutal son of a bitch,

Dot, but you've got to remember I gave her a roll of bills every week that'd choke a horse, and the sky was the limit. She got her powder blue Plymouth as a wedding gift, and then three years later she got her red Cadillac convertible. I had the printing business tied up, or thought I did, and she could have what she wanted. I even got her a sable coat with a hood, and she looked like a movie star in it. Hettie didn't care because Bennett's Furs was gone. She had the best clothes in town 'cause I'd go with her when she picked them out.

"If we went anywhere special, there'd often be a photographer and a picture in the paper that said: *Edgar Clarke, owner of Clarke's Printing, and his gorgeous wife, Angela Clarke.* She'd be there, showing all her white skin and cleavage, with a pound of red lipstick and that mop of hair piled on top of her head—smoking as usual—and I knew every man in the place wanted to screw her, and I couldn't wait to get home and beat up on her little ass and bang the hell out of her until she yelled her head off.

"You may think that's a bad trade-off and she should have been a princess at home as well as everywhere else, but that's not the way it was. Home and away, she was all mine, and I did what I wanted, which was plenty. But I tried to make it up to her in other ways, and sometimes I did."

"Good you paid for the pain—or tried to," I said. "Angie, I'm leaving. See a psychiatrist, Edgar. Get an infusion of empathy. You're very sick, and you need help. Twenty years of analysis would be a good start."

Edgar stumbled to the kitchen, probably to get another refill. Angie saw me to the door. "He's said all this to humiliate me in front of you. He loves talking about it—it's almost as good as doing it.

"That's why I wanted to talk to you. I've got to leave him now. It's not just for me; it's for Bobby. Bobby tries so hard, and he deserves better. I'm sorry you had to hear all this, especially from him." All of this was said in a whisper that made me question her determination. I struggled with sympathy and exasperation.

"I'm sorry you didn't see fit to do it for yourself. Such a victim, Angie, and never sharing the worst of this with me so I could have helped. And I would have helped. I was your best friend, remember?"

"I've tried, Dot. I've seen a lawyer and a doctor. And you were away and had your studies. You're disgusted?"

"Among other things," I replied. Then I realized I sounded unsympathetic. I wasn't. The truth was I was horrified.

20. The Confrontation

M Y BEST FRIEND was revolted by Edgar's outpouring—
I'd allowed him to do the unspeakable. She'd never
feel the same about me. She would just feel disgust, with
perhaps some pity thrown in. She would judge me. Even
her love for me would not survive this new knowledge. My
anger and hatred for him was surfacing and choking me.
I sat next to a sleeping Bobby on the sofa.

Edgar sat slouched in his leather chair, nursing the last of a
series of ryes he'd obviously been drinking throughout the day.

I saw him like an artist would: an overweight twenty-four-
year-old who looked forty, his ample gut sprawling under his
untucked, rumpled plaid shirt, his dark hair oily and long,
and his pale unshaven face puffy from fat and rye. On the
chesterfield Bobby slept, his round cheeks still moist from
past tears. I kept my voice low, but there was an edge I
couldn't control.

"Are you happy, Edgar?" He looked at me with blurred
eyes, and then looked away. "I always knew you were
twisted—even cruel and crazy—but I never believed you were
stupid. But now you've just shown how stupid you really are,
drooling over all your dirty doings with my best friend."

"Fuck off." His voice was listless, almost indifferent.

"I'm fucking off, Edgar. I'm fucking off tonight. And after
your big confession about all the things you've done—and

some I've let you do—I don't have to worry about going to court anymore. You've confessed it all. And to a law student."

"You're too damaged. No one will want you."

"You mean my breasts, and my wrecked ass? You've done a job on my body, but at least I'm not a fat, demented bully, who frightens our little son, who's the way he is because of his father's lousy genes. What a pathetic piece of crap you are. You're twenty-four but you look a boozed-up forty, and your business is headed for the toilet. The only interesting thing about you is that you've spent the last two and a half years raping and torturing your wife, and the last year abusing your little boy."

"You never loved me—"

"No, I never did, and you knew that, and made sure I never would. But for eleven months I started to care for you. I tried to forget what you'd done. But you couldn't keep it up. Perhaps your rotten mother caused it with her spankings, or your father with his porn, but you could have done something when you saw the hurt you were causing, instead of using it as a turn on for even more hurt. You could have gotten help."

"Finished?"

"Finished."

He sat, looking ahead, and he drained his glass before speaking. "I can't live without you." He whispered it in a hoarse but audible voice.

"Then don't."

I picked up Bobby, slowly carried him upstairs, and put him in his crib. Then I took my suitcase from the closet, placed it on the bed, and started packing. I thought of that day when I'd packed for Montreal and he'd stopped me at the airport. Nothing would stop me now. I heard him coming upstairs, and for a moment he paused at the bedroom door, and then continued on to the bathroom. I heard the door close.

I kept packing.

21. A Final Goodbye

I SHUFFLED THROUGH THE SNOW of the neglected pathway and walked across the street, so disturbed that I was oblivious to the cold. My mind was heavy with torment and with the guilt I felt for not detecting what had been happening sooner. Did my absorption in my own future law career prevent me from realizing what was happening to my closest friend? The sun was gone, and darkness was falling across the snow, where the spruce trees cast their purple shadows. I tried to make sense of the situation.

It troubled and shocked me that Angie had stayed and had a child with this man. Did she believe that she was of such little value without Danny that she deserved the pain? I wished she had loved herself as much as she loved Bobby. And why didn't she tell me? And worse, why didn't I detect it? And why did Edgar suddenly make these revelations?

"Our neighbourhood sexual sadist has been bragging to me," I informed Wills when I got home, not seeing Ma, who was sitting peeling potatoes on newspapers at the kitchen table.

"What's a sexual sadist?" she inquired.

"Someone who enjoys inflicting pain through sex." I saw Wills shaking his head at me. What was his problem? Ma was over fifty, and I couldn't let her level of sophistication stop at this age.

"Oh," crowed Ma, "how dreadful. No wonder dear little

Angie cut her honeymoon short. Don't you think Hettie should be told?"

"She's leaving him, or says she is. Don't breathe a word of this to anyone."

The grin on Wills's face incensed me so I tossed him a look that could singe his eyebrows. I trotted upstairs and he followed me.

"Edgar's drunk and crazy, and he described to me what he did to Angie on their honeymoon and later—God knows why. I'll be her witness if it gets to court—which of course it won't because of her ridiculous reluctance to expose him." I saw Wills waiting for details, but he wasn't getting any. I was furious with Angie for putting up with Edgar, but this didn't cancel out my loyalty.

"I told you he was a sick fuck—he got off on telling you. Do you want me to go over there?"

"No. She finds it all shameful, even with me, and I'm her best friend. I don't understand why she didn't tell me all this before. It hurts me. But I should have seen what was happening. I can't forgive myself for that. I should have helped her."

I made supper, trying to distract myself. I hoped Edgar had passed out and that Angie had postponed telling him of her decision to leave until he was sober and someone else was present. Perhaps she should just leave and have a lawyer's letter delivered. Some women did that.

"It's a bad scene over there, Ma," I said, flipping over flour-covered cod tongues, sizzling in pork fat. "He's drunk and nasty."

"She should leave," said Ma firmly. "Even Hettie thinks she should leave."

"If Hettie knew what was going on, she'd carry her out of the house—after shooting Edgar. But perhaps she knows more than we think."

"Want to see a movie?" Wills asked. "It'll take your mind off things. Betty Grable and Victor Manure are on at the Paramount." Wills couldn't stand musicals.

"I'm reporting you to Victor Mature's lawyer for slander," I retorted. "You're just jealous because he's so great-looking."

"Did you hear that, Pop? asked Wills. "Another ground for my future divorce. Mental cruelty, caused by my wife's gushing over movie stars and further damaging my already battered self-esteem brought about by her marks."

Before anyone had time to laugh, there was a brisk knock on the door. Wills opened it, and Hettie stood there without a hat or coat. She was huddled there in the cold in just a housedress, the porch light shining down on her thinning grey hair and sharp, pale face. "Dorothy, Angela wants you right away. Edgar's had a heart attack. I told her she must phone for an ambulance. She said no. She only wants you."

I don't remember crossing the street, but I must have, because suddenly I was at the door and Angie was opening it.

"Your mother said a heart attack—" I began. She shook her head, her face carved ivory. She took me by her hand, which was icy cold, and I went with her slowly up the stairs.

He was lying on the bathroom floor, a straight razor still in his open hand. His throat was another mouth, still gurgling blood. *Who would have thought the old man to have had so much blood in him? Who said that? Was it Lady Macbeth or Macbeth himself?* My thoughts were inappropriate and insane. Edgar was only twenty-four.

His eyes were fixed, and the blood was spreading against the tile, a crimson plume surrounding his head and shoulders. He was naked, this bear of a man, his dough-like flesh slowly becoming blue against the white tile. *Did he undress so as to prevent staining?* Another insane and inappropriate thought. His flaccid organ, shrunken in death, lay against his thick hair-packed thigh.

"He's dead. You know that, Angie."

"Mom wants to say he's had a heart attack. He's only twenty-four. Do people have heart attacks at twenty-four?" She was whispering. "He left a note." She handed it to me. It merely said, in a scrawl: *Angie, you know why.*

I tore the note up and flushed it down the toilet.

"You will say that he was depressed. He was worried about his business. He had a handicapped child, and he had a problem with alcohol. That's what you'll tell the police if they want a statement—and they will. No need to say anything else. If anyone inquires, say it was a heart attack. We'll have a closed casket. There will be rumours, but just deny them. Say in the obituary notice that he died suddenly. Then recommend instead of flowers, mourners make a donation to the Heart and Stroke Foundation. Let them come to their own conclusions. I'll phone for an ambulance and say there's been an accident."

"I'd already packed, and I was leaving, but I shouldn't have told him when he was so drunk. I hated him, but I didn't want him to kill himself. I just wanted to be left alone."

"But you never would have been, luv. He'd have never left you alone. This is the only thing that would have stopped it."

"I know that," she whispered. "That's why I didn't call the ambulance. That's why I just sat there on the edge of the bathtub for thirty minutes, watching him bleed to death."

I telephoned for the ambulance, then I wrapped my arms around Angie and rocked her. We left the bathroom and began to unpack her suitcase.

22. An Amateur Psychoanalyst and Reluctant Priest

THE HOUSE IS EMPTY and silent: the only sound an occasional scratch from the beginning of a late December snow squall clawing against the windows. Edgar's body, large and covered by a grey blanket, is gone, and is now having its throat sewn up at Kendall's Funeral Home. The once tumescent organ lies chilled against the stout thigh. Hettie swears one's anatomy is scrutinized and discussed at Kendall's prior to embalming. She will, she has instructed, be "prepared" elsewhere.

Angie and I clean the bathroom with three pails of water and Sunlight Soap, to rid the floor of blood. Two young constables arrive and leave. They appear satisfied with the cause of death as given. Bobby, stuffed with Hettie's shepherd's pie, sleeps soundly.

I sit with Angie, a bottle of Crown Royal, Edgar's favourite, on the coffee table between us. We are there to speak ill of the dead. Now, Angie wants to tell me everything and I am to listen and not show exasperation, disapproval, or disgust, or express the sentiment that it is now too late.

Outside the squall has subsided and the snow has started, big, soft, slow feathers, landing like lace on the windows. Angie is looking straight ahead. She inhales, and I see the orange button glow in the dusky room. Her face appears ravaged, as white as the falling feathers, her eyes, mauve smudges underneath, filmed, all made more obvious by the mop of rich tousled hair. She looks much older than her twenty-two years.

I feel a twinge of nostalgia. I see her walking beside me on the way back from school, her voice high and childlike, her cheeks round and rosy in the cold of winter. And I miss her laughter, the "Oh, Dottie," at my sarcastic remarks. And her enthusiasm as she waited for Danny's return. There are no more bubbling clichés. There was a disconcerting solemnity, a gravitas, which made me ache for my old-young friend, my Bowring Park swimming buddy, my walking to school mate. A reluctant and inappropriate priest, I would listen to her confession, as I had listened to Edgar's.

I hear the litany of abuse, the lawyer and doctors seen, the advice given, and the futile efforts to escape. Then Edgar's own childhood abuse, related in great detail, as if Angie had absorbed each word in an effort to perhaps provide a window of understanding into the soul of this strange and tortured man, whose jealous and raging obsession for her could be realized only through pain.

Angie speaks in a flat voice as she smokes. I let her go on. I am no longer angry, but rather, ashamed. I had not been there for her. I had not probed deeply enough. I had betrayed Danny's belief that I'd take care of her. She'd thought that I'd judge her.

I pour myself another rye. It's three o'clock but I'm not tired. Outside the windows are packed with snow and the wind is starting up again. My wonderful husband is across the street sleeping. Angie sighs and lights another cigarette. I react to what she's told me.

"Imagine every day for twelve years, and she started young. He was only a baby. It must have been so frightening for a little tyke, barely toddling around at a year, being given those stinging senseless beatings. And she was about to graduate to a wooden spoon, but she would have missed the burning skin under her fingers."

Angie sighs, starts to speak, but does not continue. I read her mind: *Dottie and her love of amateur psychoanalysis. And was I trying to justify Edgar's behaviour?*

"Thank God for Miss MacAlister and Miss Diamond, or we'd have had a Jack the Ripper on our hands. He feared rejection, but he selected you. Those honeymoon letters—Edgar knew everything in them. He watched you and Danny make love on graves. He heard you and the cooing doves in your throat, decided not to compete, and substituted screams."

"You make it sound so calculating, Dot, which makes it even worse than it was. I've never made sense of why he was the way he was, although I suspected it was connected to his mother. He wanted me to believe that. I was too caught up in the pain to make excuses for him. What bothered and bothers me are the things I let him do. Of course, no one ever accused me of being brilliant." I glance at her and give her a small smile.

"No," I say. "I believe Edgar was ready to do what he did. He'd been waiting a long time. And the sanctimonious chidings about you 'deserving it'—who does that remind you of? Margaret Clarke."

"He was so insecure. Imagine how it must have affected him seeing you hover over the baby, who he'd dismissed as damaged goods. This was all he could father—another blow after all those months of behaving himself. No wonder he stole Bobby's milk.

"This scared me, Dottie. He knew it would. I knew what he was capable of, and I already suspected the baby would have problems. I wanted to believe torturing me didn't mean he would abuse a child, although Dr. Macpherson made the connection. Edgar was already starting to bully Bobby. He'd do it just to hurt me. Then there was that Nembutal doping—proof that I was trying to murder him. But just before he cut his throat, he knew it was over. After you left, I told him I was leaving. And when he said he couldn't live without me, I said, 'Then don't.'"

Little silver slivers of dawn are leaking through the snow-packed windows of the smoky living room. It's five o'clock and my head is aching from the rye and information—information too ghastly to absorb in one single night.

"Let's try to get a couple of hours sleep. We have to be functional the next few days."

"I have painkillers," she chirps drowsily. "I always needed them."

23. A Funeral and Some Memories

A WHEEZING ORGAN PLAYED "Abide With Me" in the Christ Chapel of Kendall's Funeral Home, with its narrow stained-glass windows and its scent of roses and hyacinths. At the front of the chapel was a shiny mahogany casket, and on the lid was a spray of roses with a card: *With love from Angie and Bobby.*

"He should look nice, Dottie. Edgar would not want to look bad, even if he's not on display." We had viewed him, Angie and I, before the service, in his dark grey suit and blue satin tie, his throat neatly stitched. The embalmers had not been able to make him smile, and Edgar had gone scowling into eternity. "Not happy," Angie had whispered to Edgar, "you should look peaceful."

"He never was happy or peaceful."

Edgar, the abused child, haunted and saddened me. I asked myself how different he might have been. Looking at the closed casket, I saw a battered child. Angie saw a source of nightly pain and a bully to her handicapped son. Had I been Angie, I would have seen worse.

There were whispers that it was not a heart attack at all, but the charade continued throughout the service. Reverend Dr. Musgrave of the Anglican Church rightly acknowledged that Edgar had gone "much too young." He assured the congregation that Edgar had been extended Christ's infinite mercy and was undoubtedly being welcomed to a specially prepared place.

Full of little brunettes ready to be ridden around the track, I thought. Then I remembered, Edgar only hurt the one he loved.

There were some complimentary eulogies. One of his workers spoke of his outstanding work ethic and another of his generosity to his employees. He was a member of the Lion's Club, the Freemasons, and the Shriners and had not hesitated in donating money for crippled children. Sexual sadism aside, his conduct in every other way appeared highly commendable.

After the service, Angie approached me with a grey-haired woman of about fifty. "This is Miss MacAlister," she said, "Edgar's kindergarten teacher."

"I feel terrible about this," Miss MacAlister murmured. "I loved Edgar. He was such a dear little boy, so anxious to please. I always felt things were difficult for him at home. I remember the class having a conversation about what happened to them after school. Most of the students talked about playing or having milk and cookies with their mothers, but Edgar said, 'I get spanked.' The children all giggled, as children will, and I said, 'But surely not every day Edgar?' 'Every day,' he replied sadly. He was so resigned to it. Later on I asked, 'Why are you spanked?' He merely said, 'I'm bad.' It was then I assured him he was a wonderful boy and not bad at all. But I was only his teacher for a year and could hardly undo what was being done. Mrs. Clarke was a very strange woman. I was so happy when I heard how successful his business was and that he'd married Angela, who was the prettiest—and sweetest—girl in the school. I said to myself: Edgar overcame that nasty beginning."

The Spoon Lady, Margaret Clarke, sat with her daughter Shirley, her dark, button-like eyes dry and alert, her lemon-coloured face a shrivelled map of spite and malice. She took my arm and rasped in a halitotic whisper: "If your friend had treated him better he'd be here today. She should never have married him. He died of a broken heart. He was so generous, but she didn't care. He spent all his savings on that cruise, jewellery, and two fancy cars. She never appreciated it, not at all. She wouldn't even go to Paris on their honeymoon when he'd prepaid for the trip."

I had a dozen responses in my head, each one more vicious than the next, but merely said, "Perhaps you should search your own conscience when it comes to your son."

"I don't know what you mean, but be sure to get the dirty magazines out of the printing office before you sell it." Shirley, who'd at least shed some tears throughout the service, pulled her away.

I wondered if this was convenient amnesia or rationalization for her years of cruelty. I moved away, unable to bear her presence any longer.

I drove Angie back to our house in Pop's Lincoln. Hettie was caring for Bobby, and Wills had not attended the funeral—he'd said he hadn't really known Edgar, but that he knew enough about him not to attend his funeral. Ma also stayed home—she'd said that preparing a dinner that would include Angie and Bobby would be of more practical benefit than sitting through a funeral service.

Angie's mood was a mixture of guilt and relief. "Do you think things would have been different if I'd loved him?" she asked me.

"He needed more help than you could ever have given him. Besides, unless you're ready for sainthood, how could you love someone whose best moments were spent having you cry out in pain? His mother hooked him on pain and sex. I don't want to hear any more of this garbage."

"I really hated him toward the end. The two months while I recovered and then the nine months of pregnancy made me realize he could control his impulses."

I shook my head. "It's not as simple as that, Angie. I'm not so sure he could control his impulses. You keep seeing him as a normal person, but there was nothing normal about Edgar. By the time he married you, or most likely years before, he was a sadistic, insecure human who needed a lot more help than you could ever have given him. It's too simple to merely say he loved to cause pain."

"I say simple things because I'm simple. I'm no intellectual, Dot. You know that. I wanted very simple things, and I feel cheated that I didn't get them. I feel bitter, and I wish I didn't. When I saw Edgar lying naked on the bathroom floor in a pool of blood, when I saw that organ of his lying against his leg, all I could think of was all the pain it had given me and that now it couldn't cause any more damage. That was terrible of me."

"Not really. Not terrible at all. Really quite human, unless you're the masochist Dr. Gervais asked about. I'm quite relieved to hear you say something like that. I used to worry about you accepting what he did. I would have poisoned him with small daily doses of cyanide."

"I did give him Nembutal to knock him out."

"Perhaps not enough. By the way, he's left you everything in his will, and I'm the executor. You'll be very comfortable. You can sell the business or hope it's taken over by a mainland firm."

"I'm keeping the house only because it's across the street from you and mom. Edgar was supporting his mother and sister, and I suppose I should continue to do it."

"We'll set up a trust fund and pay out the interest to them. And we can make Bobby the residual beneficiary. I feel sorry for Shirley, but the Spoon Lady is a horrid sick bitch. She no doubt has her own story too. I just hate her for the way she got her revenge though: brutalizing a defenseless little kid."

Angie sighed. "That's what finally did it for me—the way Edgar treated Bobby. There were all sorts of reasons and excuses for Edgar's behaviour, but I was left with the end product. I stopped nursing Bobby at seven months, but I had to keep my milk supply for much longer because Edgar insisted on draining my breasts every night. He wanted to one-up his little son, but he was probably also making up for the fact that Margaret Clarke found breastfeeding disgusting. God, how I've suffered because of that bitch."

I was astonished. This was not the sweet, acquiescing Angie I knew. Perhaps if pushed enough even Angie would retaliate. And there was more.

"Don't worry about money. Mom has a big trust fund for Bobby. She's got piles of money stashed away. Do you know what she said to me yesterday? 'Angela, we make so many mistakes in life. If I were to do it over again I'd be a more tolerant and better person.' I know she was thinking of Danny, but it was too late for all that."

Angie's outburst in the Lincoln while coming back from the funeral did not herald a new more resilient and realistic Angie as I had hoped. It was, unfortunately, more like a last hurrah. As the day wore on, she became quieter, almost listless. She merely picked at the roast chicken dinner, which distressed Ma. "Eat up Angie, I cooked it just for you," Ma coaxed, but Angie merely smiled her appreciation.

"Come over with me. I don't want to be alone," Angie whispered when we had finished our dinner. I hoped that she was not slipping into a depression again. There were no tears, as with Danny, and surely her feelings about Edgar's demise must be at least mixed. It was unsettling to find your spouse's bloody corpse minutes after you told him you were leaving, even if your exodus was more than justified. And it was disturbing to hear such laudatory eulogies about him, and then to talk with the very individuals who had born witness to his disturbed childhood. But I could not sacrifice another year providing solace as I had with Danny. Angie was on her own; however, as long as I remained, I'd do what I could.

Wills had heard Angie's whisper. "Guess I'll spend another night at the bar at the Newfoundland Hotel with my buddies," he reported cheerfully, clearly relishing the prospect. "All the sacrifices I make for you girls."

"I suspect he's in with a bunch of Irish drunks," muttered Ma as she removed the dinner dishes. "Some say the Scottish are worse than the Irish."

24. After the Funeral

ANGIE'S DARK HOUSE SMELLED of stale smoke, rye, and death—like a multitude of dried rose petals. The half-empty bottle of Crown Royal from three days before was still sitting on the coffee table, along with our empty glasses and an ashtray overflowing with cigarette butts, some with red ends. Bobby toddled aimlessly around and plucked one from the ashtray.

"No, no, Bobby. Don't touch." Angie's voice was as empty as the silent house. Outside, the white remnants of Monday's storm stood crisp as paper against the icy air and frozen grey sky. Bobby dropped the butt on the carpet, but then he picked up another and looked at us inquiringly.

"No, Bobby. Just put it back—that's a good boy," I ordered. He gave me a slight smile and dropped the second butt on the carpet.

"Beddie-byes, Bobby," Angie sang, with an edge of impatience. She looked at me and said, "I don't even want to go upstairs."

I escorted Bobby upstairs and deposited him in his bed. I didn't bother with face-washing and tooth-brushing. "Want Mama," he murmured.

"She'll be up in a minute," I lied.

When I returned, Angie was sitting where I'd left her, a new cigarette in hand. Her face was ashen, the smeared smudges under her blurred eyes adding to the appearance of a terminal malignancy. Against her grey face, the surviving traces of her crimson lipstick appeared inappropriate, almost ghoulish.

"I can't face staying here, getting rid of his clothes and everything else. Too much has happened in this house. I'd sell it, but it would be stupid with both our mothers across the street and you here on holidays. I'm so tired, so drained. My body's been sucked, chewed, bitten, banged, and pounded—there's nothing left. I'm used toilet paper, discarded in a fall garden, ready to dissolve when the next rain comes."

Yes, she's depressed, poetically so. Worse, she had cooperated or at least acquiesced with her torturer, now lying in frozen ground at Mount Pleasant Cemetery. *Not pleasant, to be lying at Mount Pleasant in your nice grey suit and blue satin tie. All dressed up with no place to go.*

"Perhaps you should sell it. If Wills and I come back here, I don't know where we'll live. Why not have Willy and me clean out some of Edgar's things tomorrow? You and Bobby can go shopping and have lunch out."

The phone rang.

"I can't talk to anyone."

I sighed and answered. She was making it difficult for me to leave, but this time she had Bobby. I hung up the phone.

"It was George Drover from Clarke's Printing. There are two messages. One from Gladys Morecombe—remember her from school?—And the other from Andrew Cunningham, who was at the funeral. I always thought he sent you the best valentines at Prince of Wales." Angie sighed, lit another cigarette, and looked into the exhaled smoke.

"Tell Gladys I'll phone her, but don't say anything to Andrew. There'll be no more relationships. Everything I found joy in with Danny—the physical things—was shredded by Edgar. I can't think of sex without feeling sick. He killed himself, but long before that he killed me, that physical part of me that was open and loving. Too many rides around the track and too much pain. The stallion's dead, but he killed the filly first."

Edgar would have been pleased.

I reached for Angie's small, cold hand.

25. Cleaning Up

WILLS AND I CLEANED out Edgar's things together. There was pornography in the basement, including some magazines with the more violent pictures marked with folded and dog-eared corners. We threw them in the furnace. "I'm glad we did this and not Angie," I said. "She's having a hard time coming to terms with what she allowed Edgar to do. These works of art wouldn't help."

Upstairs there were dozens of expensive suits hanging in immaculate shape in the bedroom closet, together with sports jackets, trousers, and overcoats. "The best labels and a lot of cashmere," I murmured. The drawers of the walnut cabinet were full of shirts and sweaters, with racks of ties hanging nearby. "Willy, these suits are just your size—or would be with some very minor alterations. Angie said they cost Edgar thousands of dollars. You don't have a good suit. You had to rent one for our wedding. They're really too good to give to charity. You'd look marvellous in them, and you'd wear them when you start working or for special occasions."

"Nope."

"Why not? Surely you're not like some members of certain Islamic sects who believe when you wear someone's clothes you absorb his essence and develop his personality. I'm not one bit worried about you becoming a sexual sadist."

"Good of you." He was grinning, no doubt trying to lighten

up what we'd found to be the depressing job of clearing out Edgar's basement memorabilia ... and yet.

"Willy, I know I've no comparisons, but I want you to know you're a wonderful lover, really wonderful... for me in any event. And you're exactly the right fit—exactly. There's nothing about you I'd change, nothing, including your size, technique, and—believe it or not—smell. In fact, every day I feel so grateful for having you in my life."

"No need for this. I'm not sexually insecure," he said. But he was smiling, obviously pleased. He placed a sturdy arm around me, hugged me, and kissed me lightly on the cheek.

"I know that, Ducks. That's not why I told you about how I feel about you—and us—sexually. Edgar made everything so dirty and awful. Angie says she never wants sex again, and I believe she means it. But what's that to do with thousands of dollars of suits and accessories? You're always worrying about money. This would mean you wouldn't have to buy another shred of clothing for ten years."

"Sorry. Can't do it. The guy made me sick, and there are things I'd be reminded of every time I pulled on his pants."

We donated the clothing to the Salvation Army, who were happy to collect it. The poor of St. John's were magnificently dressed, courtesy of Edgar Clarke.

It was strange that Wills would spend his life in khaki pants and his army shirts rather than Edgar's costly garb. He was always so concerned about finances, yet he bought me that ring—a really expensive one. Priorities, I guessed.

We went downstairs, got fresh glasses from the kitchen, and poured ourselves a shot each from a fresh bottle of Crown Royal. Willy started kissing me again, and one thing led to another. When we finished, Wills said, "Did it ever occur to you that I just might seem good in comparison to Edgar?"

Oh Willy.

26. Personal Choices

I HUGGED MA, POP, ANGIE, and Bobby, who was a sweet affectionate little boy. We headed out four hours late in slight flurries, driving to Halifax to complete second-year law. Classes started at nine the next morning. "I sometimes think," I said to Wills, "that Angie's life is right out of a gothic novel or even a horror movie. Just think of it. She loses her real love during the war, and then she marries a sadistic brute who not only sodomizes her on their honeymoon, but beats her unconscious. As well, he uses his bird to torture her throughout the marriage—I saw it on the day of the suicide."

"Do you ever listen to yourself?" snarled Wills. The back seat was loaded with items placed there by Ma and Angie. "All useless," he had proclaimed, and it would fall to him to drag them up to the second floor, bad knee and all. Besides, I had kept him waiting for hours while I drank tea and gossiped with Ma and Angie. "The man has cut his throat and bled to death, and you're eyeing his dick. How sick is that?"

"It's just that I'd heard so much about it."

"This is what men call locker room talk, but it's between two women. I thought you girls were better than that."

"You don't understand," I said. "Edgar told me some of it himself. You're being very unfair to Angie. She didn't even confide most of this until much, much later and some of it after Edgar's death. One look at her little bruised bottom and

I'd have gone over with a knife and severed all that equipment or had you knock him about."

"What makes you think I'd buy into any of this? I find your friend, your best friend no less, complicit in this bloody, bizarre scene. What woman is going to put up with what was done to her? He should have been charged with two counts of assault causing bodily harm."

"Willy, there isn't even divorce here. And what makes you think she'd get that much sympathy? There are no women judges. She's not an aggressive woman, and he exploited that."

"Whatever," growled Wills, lifting both hands off the wheel in frustration.

The flurries were becoming worse, and the wipers were building up masses of snow on the sides of the windshield. We were leaving late, which meant our schedule was shot. It was all my fault for sitting, drinking tea, and chatting with Ma and Angie.

"Angie's giving Edgar's mother and sister the interest from the Clarke's Printing sale; I suspect it may be quite a lot. I thought that was so generous, considering the mother's attitude at the funeral. I could charge an executor's fee, but of course I won't, seeing it's Angie."

"Why the hell not? Take it off the sale of the business. Let Edgar's mother take the fall. Maybe then we can cut down on handouts from Pop. I gave him a promissory note for that last advance. I insisted on it. Fucking embarrassing, taking money from Pop, after that big wedding gift. I'm glad I'll be doing criminal work. In civil litigation, you run into all sorts of crap with the public, people doing crazy things like Angie giving away estate money. I'd rather prosecute or defend a crook any day; at least you know what you're dealing with. And speaking of crooks, I can't believe those military bastards, cutting us off like this. Not worth losing my knee for." Wills was in a foul mood. I should have kept quiet. We never fought and this was a nasty first.

"Yes, the military is terrible. They can't even supply decent condoms. Those antique things we had probably went on every war mission." I was referring to a pre-Christmas accident, a breakage, after we had celebrated writing a final mid-term during the last week of November.

"You did a follow-up on that?" A military man: the sergeant. I was to follow up to avoid possible enemy attack. He was referring to a proposed precautionary douche I had intended to take but had fallen asleep.

"Of course, Sergeant," I lied.

"That would finish us off. You'd have to quit law—you know that."

Nothing would ever make me quit. I could hear Professor Dryden's voice, dry, precise, and British, addressing the class at the end of the term: *There's a reason why we don't welcome female law students. Their personal choices make their training a complete waste of time.* Professor Dryden, forgetting my A in contracts in a heartbeat. I would not let the side down by becoming a pregnant female dropout. The Angies of the world needed me.

It was all hypothetical in any event. The date was wrong. It would be impossible.

"We could sue the military for issuing defective condoms," I chirped, trying to lighten things up.

"Sometimes I wonder about you, Dot. Nothing funny about that."

We barely made the *SS Kyle*, which transported cars and passengers across the gulf from the island to Nova Scotia. Everything Wills feared about our journey happened, and when we arrived at the apartment in the middle of a freezing night we hadn't spoken for an hour. Everything in the back seat remained there, and I didn't open my mouth. There was a class at nine.

By the third class, corporate law, we had made up. Wills brought me a coffee and half a muffin from a coffee house outside the campus. I guessed he ate the other half. "Sorry to have been such an irritable bastard yesterday, but you've got to take some responsibility. You get a real cavalier attitude sometimes—time means nothing to you. What'll you do if you have to appear before a judge and you're an hour late because you've been drinking tea with a friend?

"And I'm not as lacking in sympathy for your little friend Angie as I sounded yesterday. Sometimes I show sympathy by getting mad. It really disturbs me to hear about stuff like that, especially when the puke's dead and there's nothing I can do."

"You're forgiven. Everything you say is correct. It's all my fault, and I should be the one apologizing." This was all unfortunately true.

We returned to our miserable house, where our first-floor tenants, who had avoided rent for two months, were nowhere to be seen. Wills dragged all the pots and pans Angie and Ma had given us up the stairs, in spite of his bum knee, refusing my guilty offers to help. We opened a tin of baked beans and had a slice of Ma's fruitcake for dinner, fruitcake that had survived twenty-four hours in the back of our freezing car. And we tackled corporate finance and tax. Later, much later, we made love. Wills had purchased some new Sheiks from Connor's Corner Drug Store.

"Can't trust the military," he complained. "Those others were probably left over from the First World War. Could have been a nasty situation."

"Do you suppose," I asked, "that someday we'll look back on all this with nostalgia when we're in a really nice home—a home with a garden and a refrigerator instead of an ice-box—and think of this as one of our happiest periods?" I watched the red neon sign blink on and off across the street as we lay sweaty and cozy in our squeaky old bed with its faded quilt.

"I hope to hell not," mumbled Wills. "Things gotta be a lot better than this."

It was the middle of January 1948, and my period was late. I tried to think of any reason but the obvious one. Perhaps, I told myself, it was witnessing the aftermath of Edgar's suicide or the stress of second year. All of it could have played havoc with my hormones. I took up badminton and calisthenics for women. The latter, as women were categorized as non-athletic, was something new at the university's physical education centre. Nothing happened.

"Getting yourself in shape, sweetums?" crooned Wills. He'd been sweeter than sweet since our frosty trip back from St. John's.

I merely said, "Hmmm."

I continued with the five-member calisthenics class, and I started doing sit-ups. By the middle of February, I found that unless I ate something, anything, I'd want to throw up all morning. I settled for dry toast and jam and a cup of tea with sugar and milk. I was so tired in the afternoons I couldn't take notes—none that made any sense anyway—and I was glad Wills was in most of my classes, even though his notes were inferior to mine. The only classes we didn't share were Advanced Criminal Law, which he needed, and Family Law, which I was taking because of my interest in helping women.

Wills thought little of family law. "I'd rather get my teeth pulled out one by one without anesthetic than get into that cesspool."

It was the end of February, and my boobs were as tender as could be. At least now I have boobs, I thought.

"Strange," Wills said, after one of our lovemaking sessions, "you seem to be gaining weight in spite of all the exercise."

I felt like saying something, but papers were due the second week of March and I had two tests coming up. At times, I thought of seeing if I could stop the process, but then I thought of Angie saying so long ago, "I would never give up Danny's baby." Of course, I told myself that at this point it was only a sophisticated blood clot. Then I remembered Angie praying over the blood clot that she said she and Danny had made. My heart ached for Angie—and for myself. I knew I couldn't get rid of it; it would haunt me. Besides, I thought, the baby might be an Einstein or discover a cure for cancer. I'd heard somewhere that boys had their mother's brains. Not that there was anything wrong with Willy's brain. But mine was first rate legally, if not in any other way. But why did I keep thinking of *it* as *he*?

I waited until the mid-term tests were over and the papers complete. By then it was the end of March. We didn't drive home for reading week. The snows had stopped, but the rain had not. And there was still no sign of spring.

I went to the university's medical services. They referred me to an obstetrician named Dr. Kerr, a completely bald fellow known fondly as Curly Kerr. He looked, I imagined, like most of the babies he'd delivered.

Dr. Kerr, after an examination and a so-called rabbit test, confirmed what I had been pretending not to believe—I was about four months pregnant, and I knew the very moment of conception. *It* was due at the very worst time: the beginning of the third and final year of law school. "I kept hoping for a benign tumour," I said.

"Hardly," said Curly Kerr, not even smiling.

I made a reservation at Fat Frank's, one of the better Halifax restaurants. I could see Wills was puzzled. *Fat Frank's, even though we're chronically short of money?*

I waited until the dessert course. No need to ruin what had turned out to be an excellent dinner. I ordered a brandy for him. It was a strange choice since he'd already had a Molson's with dinner. I sat back, looked at his inquiring face, and blurted out, "I'm about four months pregnant."

His face lost every bit of colour. He muttered "Jesus" fervently—it wasn't as if he were swearing, but as if he were asking for divine intervention or help. He probably felt the same as he had when he lost his knee in Normandy. He got up and trudged out of the restaurant.

I sat and waited. The waiter came and asked, "Anything else, Ma'am?" I ordered a brandy for myself, even though I wondered if pregnant women should drink. I was beginning to wonder if Wills had found an available bridge for jumping purposes when he finally came back and sat down.

"I'm not suggesting anything," he said. "I want you to know that. This is your decision. But have you thought of any viable alternatives besides doing calisthenics and badminton?"

"Yes, briefly. But it's part of you and me, and we should treasure anything that's part of you and me." I didn't mention that this was not an original thought.

I saw his eyes mist, but only for a moment, because this was former Sergeant Campbell, who didn't show emotion in public. He reached for my hand and said very softly, "That's beautiful, Dottie. I'll support you—emotionally if not financially—but you do know this is the end of your legal career as of this semester."

I nodded. Like hell it is, I thought. *It's 1948, and the first woman to be admitted to law at Dalhousie University will not drop out. No way. I will not be the one to prove Professor Dryden correct.*

Wills had said what everyone else would say: "There is no other choice."

I had not chosen this pregnancy, but there it was, fluttering around in a little bag of water in my yet-to-be-swollen abdomen. The fact that I thought of *it* as *him* annoyed me. Why not *her*? Why was I buying into this female inferiority syndrome? Was it because my sole role model for a working woman was Hettie Bennett of Bennett's Furs? *And look what happened to her daughter.*

And my sweet dear Willy, who had encouraged me to go into law in the first place, was taking for granted that I'd quit with only one year to go. But there was no other choice.

There were two more months before the finals. I doubled my work efforts. "I really respect an individual who completes each stage of a project with dedication and expertise," complimented Wills, "even if the final stage may be unobtainable. It shows a commendable work ethic. If you'd been in my platoon, I'd have promoted you to corporal."

"I appreciate that, Sarge," I replied.

Corporal Dorothy Campbell won the award in Family Law, and also got an A in Real Estate, Corporate Law, and Tax. Wills completed his year with a B-minus average. "We should switch brains," Wills groused.

"Hardly," I replied. "My life choices, as Dryden said, similar to those of many women, are against my having a legal career." But I didn't really mean it.

27. Sisterhood

IPAID A FINAL VISIT to Dr. Kerr in late May. I was showing a lot for six months. One of my more outspoken classmates asked, "Can we predict a Campbell Three?"

I vehemently denied I was pregnant, explaining, "Living on beans and wieners will do it every time."

Dr. Kerr, bald and pink-faced as ever, left the room, summoned his nurse, and handed the stethoscope to her. They exchanged glances. "Mrs. Campbell," he said, "it seems that we may have two little heartbeats here. Miss Langley also detects them."

Twins. An answer to a prayer? Not. Or is this a nightmare? Is God looking over the clouds at me having a belly laugh?

"You will probably deliver early. With twins it's not unusual. It could be as early as the middle of August, so it would be best for you be here by August the fifteenth. At times with twins we do a Caesarean, but some women still have vaginal births. I have completed several ... successfully."

"Dr. Kerr has the best hands in the business," enthused Miss Langley.

We packed, mostly clothing that evening, for our trip back to St. John's. We would both return to the apartment in August so that Wills could complete his third year and I could produce, with the aid of Dr. Kerr's fine hands, a set of twins.

I threw my remaining underwear and shoes in a clump on

top of my already-full suitcase and sat on it so it would close. Wills neatly packed his sparse wardrobe—which consisted of two pairs of pants, three shirts, scuffed loafers, and running shoes—in an orderly fashion. He frowned his disapproval at my obviously indifferent attitude to packing. I was fast losing my corporal stripes.

"Dr. Kerr detected two little heartbeats today."

Wills did not swear or plead for divine intervention as before. His deep sigh showed a resignation to life's vicissitudes, which appeared to be boundless and aimed directly at us.

"Have you informed the registration office that you won't be returning next year?"

"I'll be writing them."

Wills eyed me suspiciously. I believe he saw my pregnancy as a breach of trust and suspected I had not douched on the infamous night of the broken condom. I had denied this. I said it was thought by many medical authorities that after-the-fact douching was not effective, that it was almost equivalent to Vatican roulette, or withdrawal. This was a lie that I told myself could very well prove true.

We drove home the first hour in silence after a check-up on Pop's long discarded Ford, which showed 360,000 miles on the odometer. It coughed, got cranky, and refused to start at times, and the heater was moody. It was the first week in June, but the weather was cold and rainy as we travelled to the island. I turned on the heater, and a blast of cold air slapped me in the face.

"Lucky that the government's taking me back," said Wills. "If they want me for my articling year in '49 then they'll offer me a position as Crown. It'll be a great background for when I want to start my own defence practice. First thing I'll do with my new income is get us a new car—we'll pay it off over time. We'd only get five bucks for this one. We can't transport the twins in a car like this."

It was the first time Wills had spoken of the twins as actual living, breathing entities, worthy of being transported in a decent car, rather than disembodied, mendacious little embryos, intent on ruining their mother's career plans and their father's financial future. Now I could see them, beaming away at me in gratitude from the back seat, with their father's nice blue eyes and square jaw and my fine legal brain firmly ensconced in their curly blond heads.

I plucked up his large rough hand with the fine light fuzz on the back and gave it a resounding, smacking kiss. "You're wonderful. You know that, don't you?"

"In comparison to some, I'm bloody terrific."

The crossing of the gulf was rocky, and then the Ford wouldn't start. We borrowed some cables for a boost and finally set off for Ma and Pop's in St. John's. We drove past dozens of small outports, their brightly painted box-like homes clinging to the coast, while the harsh grey Atlantic lurched angry against the seamed, granite rocks.

"Ma'll die when she sees me. Pop will be torn between his pride about my becoming a lawyer being dashed to pieces and his joy about becoming a grandfather—to twins."

"You could have told me," Ma sniffed, as she removed a lusty, strong-smelling roast, leaking red, from the oven.

"I didn't even tell Willy for four months, which was when I was officially notified by the doctor. I didn't really want to believe it. It wasn't as if we planned it. It was an accident—I'll spare you the details. You don't believe I've worked this hard for two years at law school to have this happen, do you? I was considered a forerunner for women, and I've let everyone down. Willy says I've got to notify them. They may have a male substitute take my place for third year—someone, as one of the professors says, who won't waste their legal education by making 'wrong personal choices.' Not that choice had anything to do with this." Ma pursed her lips in thought.

"Too bad, Dottie. And your marks were wonderful—better than Willy's, right?"

"Better than Willy's, but he'll probably make a better lawyer. He's more grounded, sane, down-to-earth, and disciplined—he's military guy, after all. The best lawyers are like that—with B averages." Ma added a scowl to her pursed lips. She wasn't listening.

"Dottie, Dottie, darling, darling."

It was Angie coming in the front door. She was thin and pale, and her piled thick mound of hair emphasized a face chiselled in ivory. *Too much pain, too much hurt. The beloved and the tormentor are gone, but both have left their mark on that face with the still-luminous green eyes.*

Bobby stood beside her smiling a welcome, his face just like Angie's in the old days, the days before Danny and Edgar, when we walked together back and forth to Prince of Wales College over sidewalks packed with snow. He was immaculately dressed, from his jaunty cap to his tweed overcoat and his beige suede boots.

"How are you, Bobby, sweetheart?"

"Good," he whispered shyly, glancing at Angie, who nodded approvingly.

"You're preggums!" This, with a shriek, from the owner of "going to the little girl's room" and "taking a pee-pee." I had missed them—those childlike clichés; so good to have Angie sounding like her old self again.

"Unfortunately."

"Don't say that—it's wonderful! Aren't you thrilled?"

"Angie, think about it. I'm entering third-year law, and now I've got to withdraw and parent what they believe are twins."

"Twins!" A chorus from both Ma and Angie.

I saw Angie biting her lower lip as she always did when thinking deeply.

"Boots," said Bobby. I was puzzled.

"You have your boots on. He wants to help you take them off."

"How very kind," I said to Bobby, extending a foot as I sat in one of Ma's wooden kitchen chairs. Bobby, his face serious with the effort, pulled off my scuffed suede boots, trotted off, and deposited them by the front door.

"He'd love to help you put on your shoes." Bobby returned with Ma's slippers and proceeded to carefully slip them on, on the wrong feet. I had a slight bruise on my instep. He bent over and gave it a small kiss. "We kiss bruises better," explained Angie.

"He's a wonderful little boy," I said sincerely, blinking hard. But I wondered what fodder he'd make for the class bullies, this diligent little man.

"I'm going to Pop's office anyway," I told Wills within a week of our arrival. "It's the least I can do after the way they've helped us. Pop says I'm a great help there. Ma and I will drive each other crazy if I stay home."

"It's up to you," said Wills. "Don't see much point in it, but it's your decision. Have you written to the registrar?" Ever since the pregnancy, I sometimes got the feeling that Wills didn't trust me.

"I have the letter half done. You never know when I might have the opportunity to return. The wording is important.

By July I was huge, but I did not miss a day at Pop's office, closing real estate deals and drafting and typing contracts. Had I not been so outrageously pregnant, I would have appeared in Family Court, where law students were permitted to represent those without lawyers.

"Too bad you can't complete law school," said Pop, as we drove home toward the end of July. "You've got the makings of a fine lawyer. But it's a woman's place to have children and stay home, I suppose."

"Perhaps you can have it all."

"Really?" asked Pop.

On July 22, 1948, a final referendum was held to decide Newfoundland's fate. The Roman Catholic Archbishop had opposed Confederation with Canada and had made his position known. The Loyal Orange Association had then warned the Protestants to resist Catholic influence. The resulting campaign between the parties was a bitter one. The result was a 52 percent victory for Confederation with Canada.

"We've lost our country," a grim-faced Hettie told Ma, as they drank tea together the following morning. "We sold it for baby bonuses and old-age pensions, although the outport people, even a few locals, may be better off. But I'll never feel Canadian."

"Ode to Newfoundland" continued to be sung at the end of formal occasions.

At the end of July, Ma and Angie asked me to afternoon tea at Angie's house. I was suspicious. I thought they might be planning a baby shower. I imagined all the female members of our old high school class bringing a multitude of small outfits, ranging in size from one month to one year, in an assortment of colours—blues, yellows, or pinks, as one never knew. A kind gesture, and another carload of items for Willy to cart up to our hideous flat in Halifax.

I mentioned my suspicions to Wills.

"Nice," he said. "It would save us the expense of outfitting the twins." Money, or the lack of it, weighed heavily on Wills. It was the Scottish mentality, I thought: oatmeal, haggis, and thrift.

"If I were working, there'd be two paycheques," I said.

"Pointless to discuss anything so obvious," he replied.

Ma and Angie smiled at me as I waddled through the door and plumped down on the nearest padded chair.

"We've given this a lot of thought," said Angie, "and we've made a decision. We're moving to Halifax next month—your mother and me. We're going to help care for the twins so you can finish third-year law. We've even got a flat in a house next to yours with a little balcony I can smoke on. There's a special preschool there for Bobby, for slow learners. Of course, it's all up to you."

Mothers. Girlfriends. There is no one like them. I covered my face in my hands and started to cry. Bobby came over and placed his small hand on my arm. I put my arms around him.

"Don't cry, Dottie," he whispered.

"Sometimes you cry when you're happy, Ducky."

"You'll have to write the registrar and revoke your withdrawal," said Wills, later on that night.

"I never sent it," I admitted.

"I suspected that. We really must cultivate a more honest relationship. I'd hate to think either of us is incapable of being straightforward. Trust is very important."

"Very," I agreed.

It's not as if I'm committing adultery; I'm just trying to have it all.

28. Having It All

O N AUGUST 17, 1948, Stuart Charles and Donald Alexander were born. Donald was named after Pop, and Stuart after Will's dad. They were six and six and a half pounds, respectively. They were not identical, but both had square jaws, big dark-blue eyes—which I was told could be subject to change—and round bald heads covering what I predicted were two fine legal minds.

It was a vaginal delivery. Stu exited in the proper fashion, but Donny came out one shoulder first, before being expertly manipulated by the fine hands of Dr. Curly Kerr to make a respectable entrance. I attempted a natural birth, an idea that was coming into vogue, and almost succeeded, except for a gasp of Trilene gas at the very end. Wills managed to stay for most of the labour, but fled at the end, stating he couldn't take anymore and was going to faint. Worse than having his knee blown off, I thought.

"You're built for childbearing," congratulated Curly Kerr. "A good-sized pelvis is helpful." I thanked him for his efforts and the compliment. Obviously being five-ten with big hips had certain advantages I'd never considered. Now, for the first time, I would have the voluptuous bosom I'd always coveted. An African undergrad had once informed me that he had been amazed by the North American emphasis on breasts, as in Africa they were thought to be less sexy than a glass of milk.

I had two weeks to attempt to get the twins on some sort of nursing schedule before classes began. Stu was a great nurser, latching on at once, but Donny was lazy and had to be jiggled and prodded into showing any interest at all. "The milk is there, but he's just not interested," I complained to Wills, who merely shook his head. The babies terrified him. He handled them gingerly, as if they might break.

"Babies do survive on bottles," ventured Ma.

"No way," I insisted, "will I shortchange my kids because of my future career."

Angie, ecstatic over the twins, said, "Later on I can give bottles. You can pump your milk before you leave." Angie loved taking care of the babies, leaving them only when she went out on the balcony to smoke. I was concerned they might bypass their scowling milk supplier for the gentle, smiling, cooing Angie.

Bobby also hovered around the babies, examining their tiny hands and feet with wonder. "Baby's hungry," he'd report, as soon as a baby hiccupped.

Bobby was enrolled in a special school, in a class of two-year-olds. "He seems to be behind the other kids," fretted Angie, "but they said he's almost normal verbally."

"They're not always right," I said. "Look how alert he is with the babies and me."

Angie just shook her head, bit her lower lip, and went out for a smoke break.

The nights were chaos. Stu usually woke up only once, took a few desultory sucks, and collapsed back into sleep. Donny, having slept and refused to nurse all day, became a screaming bundle of demands, nursing lustily for an hour and then yelling with colic, which was only relieved by gently rubbing his tight, protruding, gas-packed, little gut.

"Demanding little bugger," I complained to Wills.

"Like his Ma. Did it ever occur to you that this might all be too much for you?"

I pushed a nipple into Donny's mouth for a temporary reprieve before answering, "Whatever makes you think that?"

It was all too much. I could have occupied myself fully with looking after the twins all day, and having a nice nap each afternoon while Ma and Angie took them out in their huge pram—a gift from Angie. But it was not to be. I had chosen a different path.

Every day I would get up at seven o'clock, after having spent hours during the night nursing and comforting Donny; toss down two glasses of milk at Ma's insistence; attempt to nurse each twin; pump some milk; and grab a slice of toast, which I'd eat on the way to my nine o'clock class. Wills would pick up a doughnut and a double coffee for himself.

"It's like being in the army again," he complained. "Everywhere you look, there's bottles and smells."

Classes went on until one o'clock. I had an hour to return home, breasts bursting with milk, feed the babies—at least I could count on Stu to drain at least one swollen mammary—attempt to coerce Donny into nursing, chow down one of Ma's chopped egg sandwiches, gulp another glass of milk, and return for the afternoon classes. On Tuesdays and Fridays, when no afternoon classes were scheduled, I'd read my wills and trusts textbook or grab an hour of sleep. Was it as bad as I thought it would be? It was worse. Even with Ma and Angie doing everything they could.

"Stuart is gaining nicely," said Dr. Halton, the pediatrician who had performed the dual circumcisions after two weeks, "but Donald should be heavier."

"He won't nurse." I was full of guilt.

"Perhaps it would be beneficial if he were fed on demand, every hour. Some babies thrive on a different routine."

"I'm a law student; I can't do that," I protested. There was no doubt in my mind that I was shortchanging my babies in exchange for a legal career. My selfishness was collecting into a bag of slime and guilt sitting squarely on my head, ready to explode into a torrent of quivering, mustard-coloured baby poop.

"I always encourage breastfeeding—it's far superior—but some babies thrive on formula. Do you have help?"

"My girlfriend and mother."

"Perhaps one of them wouldn't mind giving Donald a supplementary bottle on occasion."

Angie seized on the idea with delight. Aside from his preliminary suck at seven thirty, Donny drained bottles of formula all day and slept all night—provided he had a double bottle at midnight. More often than not, he slept at Angie and Ma's flat. He much preferred Angie to me, the miserable cow, cooing with pleasure when she approached and screaming with disgust when he caught sight of me.

"It's terrible," I said to Wills one night, after Angie had departed with the smiling Donny in her arms, on the pretense that he could sleep in her and Ma's flat and not disturb me during the night. "I've lost Donny. He much prefers Angie. At least I've still got Stu, but Ma's eyeing him."

"You've still got the liquid refreshment Stu wants. Don't overreact," assured Wills. "You knew it wouldn't be easy."

"Easy," I croaked. "It's hell on wheels."

"It won't always be hell. You'll be glad later on, wait and see." *Encouragement from an unexpected source.*

The mid-term tests came and went—a C plus and a B minus. Even Wills did better. "B students make the best lawyers," he cracked, throwing my own words back at me. "Be glad you're passing."

Stu was smiling at me. He was still mine. Donny wailed in disgust when I approached but beamed when Angie held out her arms. "If I were home all day, cooing and catering to his every wish, he'd like me too," I complained to Wills.

"All set-offs," he said, "coming within the parameters of not having it all."

"I was thinking of putting Donny on solids," Angie informed

me, Donny in her arms. "I'll start with a little pablum and mashed banana, then some strained fruit and veggies. He's ready. He's gnawing at his little fists. Aren't you, sweetheart?" On hearing this, Donny bestowed on her a beatific smile, the likes of which I'd never seen.

"Perhaps," I ventured, "you could also start Stu on some solids, although he's still nursing. You don't want his brother to be twice his size and start knocking him about at age two."

"Of course I'll start Stuart on solids too—how thoughtless of me. It's just that I've gotten so close to Donny that sometimes I think he's mine. You don't mind, do you? It's so nice to have a little baby who's so responsive, so advanced. He's sitting up at four months, really straight, and he's trying to roll over. He even follows me with his eyes."

What could I say? She was happier than I'd seen her in years. Of course, she was taking over my son, but whose fault was that?

"I want you to take over Stu from Ma. She's almost sixty— this is really hard on her."

If she has both, then perhaps the intensity of her love for Donny might be diluted. Or does she have enough love to spread around? I suspected she did.

We were in our rotten little flat, in the rickety old house that we'd purchased using the fifteen thousand dollars Pop had given us as a wedding gift. It was snowing, and the red neon light advertising the bar across the street kept blinking at the upper window through the thin sheets of snow.

"You know that's what I always wanted, to have the back seat of my car full of kids, to fill up the empty pockets. Remember, I always told you that. You've given me such joy, Dottie, letting me parent Donny and now Stu. And Bobby's happy too because he loves the babies. You've been such a friend, Dottie—in every way."

She went outside in her sable coat with the hood, and I watched her light up on the balcony. I looked at her profile against the blinking neon light. I felt like crying because she hadn't deserved any of her pain. And here she was, thanking me for permitting her to take care of my twins so I could get a law degree—as if I were doing her a favour and not the other way around.

In November, after a smoke on the balcony, she came back smiling. It had been snowing steadily, white arrows against the wind, and her hood and jacket were brushed with it.

"I just saw Danny. He was walking along the sidewalk, smoking, wearing his white sailor suit—it's strange he'd have on his summer whites in this snow. I called out to him, and he waved to me, his hand over his head, but he kept on walking. I would have gone down and tried to catch him, but the babies were here, and I knew he'd be gone."

"Does this happen often?" I asked.

"Just twice before," she answered, as casually as if I'd asked her what Donny had for dinner.

29. Playing it by Ear

IT WAS A GOOD CHRISTMAS. We had our old room with Ma and Pop, except now there were two bassinettes with Donny on one side of the bed and Stu on the other. We'd hardly gotten settled when Angie appeared at the door saying she was so lonely for Donny she wouldn't be able to sleep. Wills and I exchanged glances because Donny was always the restless sleeper and constant waker-upper, while Stu slept like a stone.

We were asking ourselves what kind of rotten parents we were, farming out one of our twins so we could get a decent night's sleep. The sleep won, and off Angie went with Donny beaming away in her arms, making us both aware he'd much rather be with lovely cooing Angie, who never put him down for one minute and gave him first-class entertainment.

We all got together on Christmas Day—Wills, Ma, Pop, Will's mother, Hettie and Clement, Angie, Bobby, and the twins. After dinner, Ma played the piano. "You've got to sing, Angie," she begged.

"My throat's smoked out," Angie said.

We were all quiet after that. She looked so frail, sitting with sturdy Donny in her arms, like a dark-haired Madonna, I thought. Wills bought Bobby a train set, put it together for him, and made the little battery cars run around the track. Bobby loved that, and he sat on the floor with Wills, smiling and looking at Angie for approval. I bought him some picture books with some little pop-ups, but he got bored very easily and wouldn't repeat any words, colours, or numbers. I saw Angie watching, her brows drawn together.

"He has a short attention span, the teacher said. He can't concentrate for long."

I thought if I got him alone, I'd try again. Perhaps he was distracted by so many people. I led him into Pop's study and perched him on the desk. But no, he really couldn't concentrate. He just kept smiling at me and shaking his head. Angie entered the room quietly and stood watching us.

"Thanks for trying," she said.

"The least I can do," I answered, "after all you're doing for me."

"What I'm doing for you is saving my life," she replied.

I decided to let Donny spend the nights at her place, although I did visit him every day so he'd know there was another woman in his life—an unimportant one—and Wills dropped over and made faces at him, so he'd know he had a daddy.

Wills and I actually did some work. The Agency and Wills and Trusts exams were in mid-February, and I also had a paper on jurisprudence to write, but decided I couldn't do it without access to the law library. I also had mid-terms in Insurance, Constitutional Law, and Evidence. I no longer aimed at towering marks. I was, after all, the mother of twins, although I was only half-parenting only one of them.

It was time to leave St. John's. I was on a plane to Halifax with the twins, and Angie and Bobby. Angie and I each held a twin. Wills was driving Angie's Cadillac—the back seat was full, as usual—with Ma in front. It was pointless to take two cars to Halifax, especially when one was almost inoperable.

Donny was fussing as usual. He was such a spoiled little guy, demanding constant entertainment from Angie, while Stu slept like a rock in my arms, full of breast milk, not to mention the mashed banana and pablum that Angie had fed him.

I was lost in thought. *Would a breastfed baby be healthier and more resilient than one who was given formula, solids, and boundless love and entertainment by the birth mother's best friend?* It would be an interesting study for nutritionists. Questions may be asked regarding the derelict birth mother. Who was she? A law student willing to sacrifice her children in order to have a professional career? I imagined my grinning photo with a question underneath: *The New Woman?* There would be stones or praises, but mostly stones, from letters to the editor depending how he or she felt about women becoming lawyers.

We had ascended into blue territory, and outside white puffs of absorbent cotton floated by the plane. Angie sat by the window, and I watched her draw a cotton blanket carefully around Donny's already bonneted head to help withstand drafts. He was a pretty baby with a pronounced rosy pout and long, dark, curved eyelashes and sparse dark fuzz just beginning to grow around his forehead. His brow was furrowed, as if he was concerned the future may not be as good as he predicted, or would in fact, demand.

Stu, on the other hand, lay complacent and leaden in my arms, his brow smooth, a smile of satisfaction—or was it gas?—hovering around his mouth. He was Willy's boy. But Donny, I thought, may have his mommy's former fine legal mind, a mind that had now gone to mush—or pablum.

Bobby was kicking the seat in front of him. I thought he was bored, and I asked him to stop.

I watched Angie as she watched Donny. At twenty-four, Angie looked much too fragile; her white skin translucent, tissue-paper thin; the small pale blue veins of her temple sketching a pattern. And, as usual, she shared Donny's furrowed brow.

"You don't look well," I said. "Are you okay? You should stop smoking. They're doing studies on it now—it could be dangerous."

"I'm fine. I just spot a lot. I'll see a gynecologist after your exams."

"How long has this been going on?"

"Forever. It's chronic. It started up again after Bobby. I was waiting for you to finish your exams."

"Angie, do you want me to die of guilt? Because I will, you know." She gnawed at her lower lip and gave me a little smile.

"Just make an appointment, Dot, and I'll go."

I did and she went. The diagnosis: cancer of the uterus. It had not metastasized. A hysterectomy was scheduled for the second week of February, study week, a week of Donny screaming for Angie, a week of him refusing to nurse or take a bottle from me. Finally Wills prevailed. Donny took a bottle, but only from Wills, and some pablum from Ma.

"He hasn't bonded with me. I'm just some hulking stranger lurking in the darkness, carrying strange potions and poisons." Wills laughed.

"He'll come around. A baby would prefer Angie: an adult would choose you."

"What a shame Edgar took his own life—I would have much preferred killing him. I wish Angie had opened up to me. I'd have gotten her out after the honeymoon. Now she'll never have more children, and that's all she ever wanted: Danny Flaherty and the backseat of her car full of kids. Instead she got the world's worst sexual sadist and little Bobby, plus my crankiest twin. Whoever said life was fair?"

Wills didn't answer. The whole Angie-Edgar scenario drove him mad.

I passed and graduated with a straight-B average. Wills had a similar average, but with an A in Evidence. There were two articling offers for Wills from Halifax law firms and one from the criminal section of the Newfoundland Department of Justice. There were no offers for me. Women lawyers were not in fashion, so it was back to Pop's office. We'd write the bar exams the following year.

"We should write them for both provinces," I suggested. "It'll give us options."

Wills shrugged. I suspected he had wanted to take one of the Halifax articling offers, the offer from the large firm that seemed really eager to have him. They had even taken him to Fat Frank's for rum and cokes before making the offer. His mother would not be that far away. She complained that she never saw us unless it was Christmas.

"You know if you want to article in Halifax, I'll understand. It's boring for you to always be with the government. I've got no other choice. No one wants me, but you're in demand. I'll understand. Really, I will."

"Trying to get rid of me?"

Men. You can't win so don't even try.

"Willy, how can you say that? Of course I want you around. It would be terrible to be without you all year. We couldn't sell the Halifax dump, and I'd have to live with Ma and Pop."

"Well then, let's not propose foolish things."

"I was trying to be nice."

"Don't. You're not used to it, so you don't do it well."

Men.

We decided we should get some help for Angie, so she wouldn't be alone with three small children all day. We'd find a nice girl from around the bay, someone who needed the money and who was good with kids. It was too much for Angie, especially since she'd had surgery in February. She seemed even frailer, more pale, her movements tentative. And now that both Wills and I were working, we could afford to pay someone. I knew it might be a hard sell, but her reaction was much worse than I'd predicted.

"Do you feel I'm not capable? Is that it? Do you feel I can't manage the twins? Do you feel Donny is too close to me? I'm sending Bobby to regular preschool. I'm going to risk it, just so I'll be free to look after the twins. They should be brought up together anyway. They can go home with you at night, as long as it doesn't upset Donny too much to leave me. And you're insulting me by offering me money. I have money—quite a lot of it. More than you have. Does our twenty-year friendship mean so little to you that you're reducing it to dollars and cents?"

"Angie, I'm only thinking of you," I protested. "You're getting it all wrong."

"We'll rent," I said to Willy. "The Reagans are both in the mental asylum. I suspected something when I saw them chasing each other with milk bottles around the yard in their pajamas. Jack Reagan has been walking up and down the street mumbling for years, and his sister Winifred has always had problems. The public trustee will rent their house to us for a hundred and fifty dollars a month, and we'll be right next to Angie and across the street from Ma and Pop. It'll be so nice, to finally have our own place."

I was as unprepared for Ma's reaction as I had been for Angie's. Clearly, I wasn't the deliverer of good news.

"Dottie, I'm hurt," Ma said. "Really hurt. Do you find Pop and me such nuisances that you want to get rid of us? For you to rent across the street—the Reagans' old hovel no less—when there's a perfectly good bedroom and bathroom at home? Is it that you feel we're invading your privacy? Perhaps Willy doesn't like us. Is that it? Pop will be crushed. He always thought so highly of Willy, like a son. It will break his heart to hear this."

I swore. A litany of four letter words, direct from the heart.

"Now I don't need to hear that kind of language, Dottie. You weren't brought up to swear like that. This is something you've no doubt picked up at law school. It's a terrible example for your dear little boys—a cursing, coarse, common mother."

"We will," I said to Wills, in a measured and even tone,

"have Angie babysit Donny and Stu. She refuses help. She also refuses money, but perhaps you could speak to her. I wish you luck. I won't discuss it with her further. I hope the twins will become attached enough to want to be together and leave Angie at night without hysterics. It would be nice if Donny could at least be cajoled into giving me a little smile or letting me take his hand on occasion. Or is that asking for too much? We'll be staying with Ma and Pop as usual. Don't ask me to explain why, but believe me: there is no other choice. Don't look at me like that, Willy. I've been called a cursing, coarse, common mother by Ma, and you say I don't do nice, so I don't want any more input from any of you—none."

"It's pointless," said Pop as we drove home from the law office together, "to fuss about something you can do nothing about."

"It's so bloody frustrating," I howled. "I try to be considerate of that damn crew, and I get nothing but abuse. Angie and Ma are the worse, but even Willy's disappointing."

"I've always found," said Pop, sighing his sincerity, "the best thing to do is to play it by ear."

30. The Bad Fifties

IT WAS JUNE 1950, and Wills and I were both writing the Nova Scotia and Newfoundland bar exams. We both passed. I was now in the swing of things, but no one really cared. Pop was hiring me to do general law and was permitting me to open my own little department for matrimonial work. He said I was going to be a great lawyer.

Wills had accepted the position of Crown with the Department of Justice, and was assisting in criminal prosecutions. He really liked it, but complained that the money was terrible. He said he was glad that Pop was paying me more than his "lousy salary." He'd made it clear that if he'd taken the Halifax offer, he'd be making more than me. Ego stuff, I feared. I reminded him that I'd suggested that he stay in Halifax to article. He snorted and said it was "a hollow offer" and "rank hypocrisy" on my part.

Life was easier here with Angie and Ma, especially now that I was working at Pop's office. Wills was popular and had his local buddies. He'd even picked up a St. John's Irish accent, which Ma had commented on—unfavourably.

Donny and Stu were almost two, and really wild and spoiled. They laughed out loud when asked to carry out reasonable requests, and fussed when they were picked up from Angie's. And a few times Donny had been so bad— giving me a sharp bite on the arm, leaving a mark—that I took him back to Angie's and told her to keep him. I thought it was the difference in parenting styles. Angie believed in distracting them if they were doing something naughty like emptying everything in sight or eating buttons or other small objects. I believed in crying "no" or "stop," which they found funny and ignored. We did have fun at bedtimes, and they were always up for hide and seek, which they found really hilarious.

On a Saturday in July 1952, we were all on Topsail Beach, which was made of smooth stones. The water was so icy our legs were numb when we dipped them in. There was only one sandy beach on the island. The rest were made of rocks and stones. It was a dull day; no rain, but the lapping water was bright grey, just showing little white tangles when it rode up against the stones. The sky was overcast, full of charcoal smudges, with just an occasional smear of white sun peeping through.

Donny and Stu, now almost four years old, were throwing stones with Bobby and periodically the twins would run toward the water until Wills yelled at them to stop. They laughed at him and attempted to continue. Bobby was almost six, and tall. He loved throwing stones, but he wouldn't run toward the water. He knew it was forbidden, and he wanted to please—a desire that never occurred to Donny and Stu.

Donny's hair had become darker, as had his eyes, and his mouth less cherubic and more determined—I noticed it when I washed his face. He had my mouth. I feared he'd inherited not just my legal brain, which I always counted on, but what some believed to be my acidic and aggressive personality—unbecoming for a woman in the '50s, but not always inappropriate for a lawyer.

At this place in time, all three boys were on the same level. That wouldn't last. I wondered if the twins would try to protect their big brother, who had already been withdrawn from school as a result of being bullied and an inability to learn.

He'd been categorized as "disruptive," and his schoolmates called him Dumbo, as Edgar had. It hurt him, although he was not sure of its meaning. Angie home-schooled him to no avail. His large green eyes, so like hers, constantly looked into space. What did he see there? Sometimes he smiled. Was it a pleasant image in this liquid space?

Angie smoked, looking out at the grey silk water with narrowed eyes. "But for the war we'd be here today. Donny and Stu, they'd be ours, but different, with Danny's black hair and blue eyes. There'd be four boys, all like Danny, and one little girl like me. On the way here, and driving back home, they'd giggle and fight in the back seat. I'd be holding our little girl on my lap in the front. Danny would be smiling, and he'd flick his Lucky Strike from the window.

"Then we'd all go to Barney's Roadhouse, and the kids would eat chips with salt and vinegar and be naughty and loud. Danny would smile and say, 'Cut it out, guys'—that's what he'd say. They'd cut it out, but only for a little while.

"Later on we'd be together, melted together in bed, and in the other rooms they'd all be sleeping. And I'd know he'd always be there."

Tears trekked down her cheeks. She made no attempt to wipe them away, but kept looking out at the grey water. It had been nine years, but he was still alive enough to inspire a fantasy, real enough to make her cry.

I would not bestow platitudes on my grieving friend. Time does not always heal. I rubbed her thin white arm and hummed my sympathy.

"Don't cry, Mommy." It was Bobby.

"Your mommy's sad. She'll be better in a little while."

31. The Invalid

I T'S 1956, AND ANGIE is not well. Donny, who is precocious and annoyingly observant, informs me, "Angie spits red when she coughs."

"Are you sick?" I ask her.

"No."

"Are you sure?"

"Yes."

"I don't believe you."

"Then don't believe me."

I seek out Hettie. She looks old; the hats and stiff perms are gone. She is no longer erect but bent over. An arthritic spine, I think. "Angie's not well, and Donny says she's spitting blood. She's lost weight and seems tired out, but won't admit it and won't see a doctor."

"She's afraid you'll take the children. She lives for your children, especially Donny. Make her see a doctor—she'll listen to you. Mention Bobby, and remind her what will happen to him if something happens to her. She worries for his future. I'm getting old, and Clement is useless since his stroke."

I go back to Angie and try again with renewed determination. "Tell me, are you spitting blood? Donny says you are. You may have tuberculosis. Now they have a cure for TB, it's no longer a death sentence. You'll need bed rest and streptomycin—

they have antibiotics now. The kids will survive, they'll be in school, and Bobby can stay with your mother. You're being stubborn. And silly."

Angie looks at me, smiles, and gnaws her lower lip. She is wearing a sleeveless blouse, and her arms are so thin my throat tightens when I see them. I leave the office early and pick up Donny and Stu at school. It is usually Angie's afternoon routine but that day I make it mine—one of the advantages of working for your father. I usually stay until five as I want the staff to take me seriously; not some lightweight, installed courtesy of Pop.

"I'll make an appointment, but promise you'll come with me to the doctor after any test results. You're better at talking to these people, Dot."

"Then sign an authorization and direction and I'll be your agent."

"You're such a lawyer, Dottie," she laughs. "I'm so lucky to have you."

Then why didn't you tell me more before, so I could have helped? But I had forgiven her. We were so different, but I understood her: her embarrassments; her reluctance to confide the shameful; her vulnerability; even her acquiescence; her avoidance of confrontation; her irrational hopes and her kindness, spontaneous and intuitive; the intensity of her love for Donny and all the children, who sit munching her crisp oatmeal cookies and drinking tumblers of cold milk.

It's a rare hot July day, and Doctor Lundrigan's office is heavy with heat. There is no air conditioning, which is redundant on an island that averages one week a year of hot days. He is of the Irish professional class, a growing East End group. Even in the West End, there are no more of Evans and his kind, and the railway houses glisten with fresh paint.

X-rays had been taken, bloodwork done, and sputum

tested. Doctor Lundrigan, heavy and red-faced, with dark sparse hair and prominent jowls, sits behind his desk. He scowls at the reports.

"Your age?" he asks Angie, who sits beside me, a fixed smile on her face.

"Thirty-one in October."

The doctor's scowl deepens.

"I'll go outside and have a smoke."

"You may smoke here, my dear," says Dr. Lundrigan, lighting up his own cigarette.

"Just speak to my friend Dorothy—I signed a paper so you could. She's a lawyer. She understands better."

Angie leaves quickly, out to the comfort of the warm sun. I feel uneasy. *She knows, but does not want to hear.* Reality, as usual, eludes her. I reach in my purse for the direction and authorization.

"No need for that, my dear, I heard your little friend. You've been on the mainland too long—we're not that formal here."

I sit and wait. On the wall, the hands of the clock point to 11:45. Time is passing, rationed out in slow relentless ticks.

"Your little friend Angela has no TB; it's far more serious than that. She has masses in both lungs and a possible invasion to the liver. She had cancer of the uterus some time ago, followed by a hysterectomy, but it appears unrelated. Her primaries are the lungs."

"Masses? Are they tumours?"

"They are."

"She smokes constantly."

"If that did it, we'd all be dead."

"The cure?"

"No cure, especially if there's a metastasis to the liver. We could radiate the lungs but only in the last stages ... for comfort. But morphine can do that as well." My mind seizes.

"Is there a specialist for this?" My voice is clotted and my eyes burn.

"A chap from the mainland—a pulmonary oncologist named Dunlop. I'll give you a referral. I suspect he'll only confirm what I've told you, but I understand you'd want a second opinion. I hate to tell you this. Only thirty-one. Any children?"

"One boy, mentally handicapped." *There's also Donny and Stuart.*

"Poor kid. Bad enough to be retarded, worse with no mother."

"How long?"

"Prognosis is difficult. It appears aggressive, so three, maybe four months. Dunlop will tell you."

Outside in the heat, Angie sits in the car with its door open, smoking. I get in the driver's seat and we drive up Duckworth Street toward the West End. We don't speak. Beyond the large, grey, stone courthouse straddling Water and Duckworth Streets, the harbour has a blue-grey sheen but between the Narrows the water appears light blue. The spruce on the Southside Hills are chocolate green, and above the Hills the sky is the same colour as the water between the Narrows. It is hard to speak of death on such a fine, bright day.

"Bad news?" she asks as we pull into the driveway.

"We'll get a second opinion."

Dr. Dunlop is intense and decisive. He orders more X-rays and redoes the original tests. His already snug mouth tightens when Angie leaves for her smoke. "Heavy smoker?" he asks.

"A chain smoker for fourteen years," I reply.

"They deny a link. Cigarettes are big business for the tobacco companies and government. I suspect a strong correlation, however. I've seen too many—all smokers. It's too late for your friend; there's a secondary tumour in the liver—a hopeless prognosis—a terrible fate at thirty-one." Dr. Dunlop was angry. I liked him for that. Anger cut away my empty sadness—and fear. "She could be hospitalized, but

I see no point in that. It's better that she's surrounded by those who love her. She'll be gone by Christmas."

Angie and I walk slowly together, along the gravel paths of the General Protestant Cemetery. The pines are tall where the twin benches sit. Are they nourished by tumescent bodies dissolving into the earth? I look at the blurred grey tombstones. *The dead have been gone so long; there is no nourishment in bones. It is appropriate that we walk here.* I hate myself for these thoughts.

"Serious?" she asks.

"Yes," I reply.

"I thought so," she sighs.

32. Saying Goodbye

THE FALL IS HARD and bright. Puffs of clouds blow across the blue sky, and in Bowring Park the leaves of large maples are turning rust and yellow. Soon the leaves will fall, golden birds to the black cold ground.

Angie sits in her bed supported by stout pillows, and picks at the food we bring her on a tray, sometimes adorned with a little vase bearing an autumn leaf or twig of spruce collected by "her boys." Hettie and Ma cook, searching for tasty treats to whet her nonexistent appetite.

"To keep your strength up," sings Ma, as unrealistic as Angie used to be.

Gaunt and grey, Hettie sighs often. Clement is half-paralyzed, and now Angie is ebbing away. Life has been unfair. She blames Edgar and smoking—no doubt in her mind that he's the cause of all this.

"But she smoked before marrying him," I protest.

"He made her smoke more," she says firmly. Hettie is no doctor, but the correlation is clear.

In the morning, I ready the kids for school. Bobby attends the same school, back in Grade 3 with Donny and Stu. He is less "disruptive" now that he's with his best friends, his brothers in spirit; he watches Stu and Donny for behaviour cues. He's ten years old and twice their size.

"Bobby can't read, not at all," sighs Stu.

"I'll try to teach 'im," says Donny sternly, "if I can get him to sit still."

At three, I leave the office to pick them up. They take over the back seat, fighting, pushing, and yelling.

On the second floor of the wooden house, Angie waits for them. They troop in and tell her of their day, registering their complaints and information. Sometimes they bring tokens of love: an amber leaf, a twig, a late fall marigold, which she accepts with thin transparent hands and smiles her appreciation.

"Angie is sick," states Donny.

He no longer calls her "Mommy" in deference to my feelings, which although not important, do exist, suspended in air somewhere in the distance.

"Yes," I answer.

He looks at me closely, his eyes, dark brown marbles, unwavering, seeking answers. Unlike the warm and smiling Stu or the affectionate Bobby, he will not tolerate evasion. Bobby is unaware of how sick Angie is, believing the bed a necessary appendage to his mother, while Stuart's thoughts are vague and cloudy, although he once asked why Angie no longer picks them up at school.

Donny waits. My "yes" does not suffice.

"How sick?"

"Very sick."

He waits. The dark eyes are unblinking, fixed.

"Will she die?"

It is not appropriate to burden an eight-year-old with thoughts of death. But perhaps he was not eight. He is too knowing: an old spirit lurking in that wiry little body with its dark head and eyes and firm mouth, not receptive to candy, save for the store-bought kind. I cannot sweeten this. When the worst happens, he will not trust me, and may not love me—ever.

"Yes. She will die."

He sighs. His head drops down, and something fine and taut, a crystal string, breaks inside him. He does not speak for a minute.

"I'll try to spend more time with her," he says softly, "and bring her more flowers."

He walks away, and I'm crying inside, both for him and Angie.

It is November: the cruellest month of the season of death. The bare brown branches of the maples are wiped clean, grey bones against a mottled ashen sky. The winds are harsh and howl against the windows of the bedroom where Angie lies somewhere between life and death. Morphine has eased the harshness of her leaving, but the ease it gives dissolves, and reality intercedes.

"Do you think there's something after? Religious people believe that."

"Probably," I lie.

"Do you think Danny's waiting for me, beneath the waves or in the clouds?"

"Yes. He's waiting."

"Are you sure?"

"I'm sure."

"Will he be angry about what I let Edgar do? Will he be disgusted?"

"He won't know. He's just there waiting with his crooked smile in his sailor suit and little cap cocked to one side. He has not moved. He just waits." She sighs.

"You're sure of that?"

"Very sure."

Ma always said that once started, lies are compounded by others. That was why lies weren't to be told. But these things have to be spoken of, and I don't know the answers. That's why I'm an agnostic, not an atheist. How could one be sure ... of anything?

"Danny came late this afternoon," Angie murmurs, "just as the shadows were becoming darker. This time his sailor suit was black, and his cap gone. He stood by the bed and took my hand, just for a moment, and his hand was so cold, but then he smiled and said, 'It won't be long now.' He's waiting, the way you said he would."

"I have a big favour to ask," she whispers. "You must speak of it with Willy. I know it's too great a favour by far, but you are my best, my only friend. It's Bobby."

"We will take Bobby."

"No, no. You must ask Willy and tell me tomorrow. Donny will watch out for him and Stuey will be kind."

Later, I talk to Wills. "It's a lifetime imposition," I tell him, "but there's no one else. Hettie's too old and a group home would not be right."

"You feel you have to ask me this? To explain it? There's no question; I've taken this for granted."

I love Willy: his bulk, his honesty, his compassion. I'm so blessed.

Angie sighs her relief and gratitude when I tell her. Danny is waiting, and Bobby is in safe hands. She trusts me and is ready.

Her children come into the room, faces crimson from the November wind. They take her hands, cool, frail, and tremulous, and Donny deposits into them his last tribute: a spruce twig.

He looks at me and I know he is aware. I look away, not wanting to meet the hurt in those dark eyes. Someday, I do not know when, I will hold him and perhaps he will love me as much as he loved Angie.

Angie drowses throughout the day and refuses food with a

slight wave of her bird-like hand. I know she's going, but my mind—and heart—rebel.

It is five o'clock, just before dawn, when the phone rings. It is Hazel Brown, the caregiver who comes at night. "She's awake, and she wants you. Her breathing's bad."

I slip from bed, dress, and enter the pewter dawn, shrouded in pale grey mist. Everything is still but my own beating heart.

I open the unlocked door and creep upstairs. Hazel Brown leaves the bedroom as I enter. Angie is sitting up against the pillows, her tangled mass of dark hair framing her ashen face. Above, the chandelier glistens.

"I had her turn on the light," she whispers. "I wanted to see you. I used to hide in that chandelier, but Edgar found out and punished me in other ways." She sighs, gives a slight cough, and continues, her voice now barely a whisper. "I've been so lucky to have you, Dottie. You saved my life twice, first in the year after Danny, and then when you gave me the greatest gift of all: Donny and Stu. Now I'm giving them back." I start to sob, and she shakes her head at me. She has counted on me not to cry.

"I didn't save you from Edgar."

"I should have saved me from Edgar. Turn off the light and stay with me, Dottie." Her breathing becomes more laboured and my sobs louder. Then the small cold hand collapses against my wet cheek.

The door opens.

"She's gone? You two was close?" asks Hazel Brown.

"She was," I say through my sobs, "my best friend."

A tearful funeral: sobbing orphaned children, the eldest not fully grasping what has happened. "Mommy is gone?" he asks. "Is she coming back soon?"

Stu places a sturdy arm around his neck and pats him comfort, although he is half his size. "She's in heaven with the

angels—Mom said so. God wanted her. It's really nice there."
It is as good as anything I can think to say.

"God made a mistake," spews Donny, angry and scowling. Angie is buried in the Bennett plot at the General Protestant Cemetery, far from Edgar, who was at Mount Pleasant. I had thought of cremation and a scattering of ashes on Topsail Beach, an innovative burial just coming into vogue, but Hettie was insistent, and it was not my place to argue.

Angie left me the house and any monies not included in the sale of Clarke's Printing. I put the money in a trust account for abused women. I hope that someday some of these women might come to me for legal help. Angie would have liked that.

33. Unhinged

WE DECIDED TO MOVE into Angie's within a week of her death. I hated the house: it reeked of pain and death. Each room I entered smelled of Angie's cigarettes. "Angie's smoking all over this house," I informed Wills.

"She was a heavy smoker, and that smoke's embedded in the house: the fabrics, carpets, even the furniture is saturated. We need fresh paint, new carpets, curtains, and furniture. This is what you smell: the residual effects of her smoking. She's not here. You're stressed by the death and all that's on your plate: three kids and a growing law practice."

Wills loved the house. It was a joy for him to move away from Ma and Pop's into new surroundings, and yet they, and Hettie, were just across the street. They were always there to take the kids at any time. And we were there for them as they aged, as they were doing, more Pop than Ma. As for convenience, the drive to our respective offices was ten minutes and to the school fifteen. I was, as usual, being difficult—if not insane.

Sometimes I heard voices that faded when I entered the room. I heard her cry out, "Stop, please stop," and then the slapping sounds and cries of pain, which echoed through my mind. There had been much suffering in this house, and in that bedroom where Wills and I slept. It hovered over me, that suffering, and contaminated our intimacy.

I could not tell Wills that. It was not rational. The dead were gone and silent, not pursuing their wretched lives and reliving each episode of horror. He slashed his throat. She died of lung cancer. Even her uterus, a site of pain and torment, was absent at her death.

Donny was quiet. He remained angry—with me, with Stu, with Bobby. He resisted Wills's reasonable requests and then complied grudgingly. It was early February 1957. Outside the snow weighed against the wooden house in frozen waves and covered the Bennett plot in the General Protestant Cemetery, where Angie slept under a thick duvet of white softness.

Was Donny mourning Angie, or was he angry with a stupid God, or was it both? And did he resent me, the inferior replacement?

It was two o'clock, early on a Saturday morning, when I heard her. This time her cries had urgency. She pleaded for mercy. From the bathroom, I heard yelps of pain and the harsh slapping of wood. I slipped from the warm bed where Wills was sleeping and entered the dark hall. The bathroom door was closed, but the light was on. I saw it reflected around the door.

"He's hurting Angie. You must make him stop." Donny stood with me outside the bathroom door. He seemed small, although big for his age. He was distressed. I opened the door of the bathroom, and it was now dark. I turned on the light to emptiness.

"We must sleep together tonight, Donny. We're both having bad dreams, so we'll cuddle and forget."

"What will Daddy think? Me sleeping with my mother?"

"He won't mind. We'll tell him of our dreams."

In Danny's bed, we cuddled close. I sniffed him. He smelled of boy: spruce, soap, potato chips, the shoes at the school's gym, and his own clean, sweet sweat. I grasped a foot. It was cold and large for a little boy. I massaged it with my hand to warm it and then the other. I wondered why this closeness was a first. And then I remembered: he was Angie's boy, ahead in all his developmental stages. He was the perfect one.

"I miss Angie. She was my best friend, and I loved her. We went to school together. She met a boy she loved. He had dark hair like you and went to war. The Germans sank his ship, and he did not come back. Later, she married a bad man who hurt her, and they lived here in this house. You and I, we were so close to Angie—that's why we dream of those bad times. Perhaps we should leave here, and then we'll think of happy times, of Angie and her sweetness and kindness, and how sometimes she made us laugh." I brushed my hand over his sharp, small face, and it was wet with tears. "Sometimes I cry for Angie too, and miss her, but we'll hold her close in our hearts."

He was sobbing and I tightened my arms. He felt so small.

"Sometimes I smell her cigarettes," he whispered.

"Yes, so do I. She smoked too much, and it made her sick. That's why she died. God didn't want her; she was too young. Now she's happy—perhaps she's with her sailor boy who drowned." I kept rubbing his feet. The cold was going. I kissed him lightly on his damp, sharp, cheekbone. "You're such a wonderful boy, so smart and sensitive. You'll watch over Bobby and Stu and be my best friend. I'm so lucky to have you. I only loaned you to Angie for a little while; she needed you so much, but now I have you back." I heard him sigh. The substitute had triumphed.

"But she was crying out for help. We both heard her."

"Just a dream, Donny, only a dream. But we'll tell Daddy we want a new house."

Later, I told Wills what happened. "You can ask Donny," I said, "he heard it too. That's why I slept with him. I hate this house, and want to move. Why live here when there are beautiful places near the sea, places that don't haunt you with memories of the past?"

"I checked with Donny," an angry Wills replied. "You've contaminated him with your neurotic imaginings—a lawyer who believes in ghosts and haunted houses. You're inconveniencing this entire family and hurting your parents, not to mention Bobby's grandmother—his only remaining tie. Don't mention a word of this to anyone or we'll never sell the place. And your clients will have second thoughts about retaining a nut for a lawyer." The sergeant—in fine, but fortunately rare, form.

Ma declared her disappointment in me once again. "I was looking forward to having you close. Pop's not well—that's why he's been staying home. He complains of headaches and seems forgetful. He sleeps in his chair all day and wakes up confused. Now you want to move and Willy says you speak of ghosts. I can't believe this—my intellectual daughter."

Wills gave in, but he was not happy. He did not hide that he believed I was indulging an overheated imagination, and he made it clear to both Donny and me, during a heated kitchen-table discussion, that not only did he not believe in ghosts, but he considered those who did to be suspect—even untrustworthy—in other important ways. Donny and I exchanged glances. The entire episode had succeeded in fostering a new bond between us, and Willy's opposition to my proposed move made it even stronger. We purchased a new home, high upon some cliffs facing Topsail Beach, and in time it was conceded that its beauty and freshness made the twenty-minute drive to St. John's well worthwhile.

And I dedicated myself to giving legal assistance to the Angies of this world.

34. The Lady Lawyer

POP WAS NOT COMING into the office, and his secretary of twenty-five years, Miss Grenville—or simply Grenville as he called her—had given me her notice, as had Ellie Brownwell, who I had always suspected was close to Pop in a more than secretarial way. I finally confronted them on the Friday afternoon of the week they'd given notice. I had made arrangements for the twins and Bobby to be delivered to Hettie's. Wills was to pick them up at five, and hopefully find it in his heart to heat up the macaroni and cheese left over from the night before, or at least prepare his fried bologna sandwiches, which Donny always referred to as "the sergeant's yuck special." I had scheduled clients for all of Friday evening.

Grenville sat looking at me, a quintessential post-menopausal, virginal, secular nun of sixty-five. She was immaculate in her grey suit which matched her hair, her sensible laced shoes planted firmly in front of her; her mouth, as firmly planted as her shoes, was closed over well-scoured dentures. Pop had once commented to me that she had a mind like a steel trap, that she could run the office without him if she wished. "Too bad," he'd muse, "she's so goddamn sour and miserable."

Ellie Brownwell was in her mid-fifties. She had coloured her hair a roaring auburn, and had black, well-tweezed eyebrows, which looked startling with her mop of orange hair. The black, I guessed, was her hair's original colour. Her mouth, with shiny bright pink lipstick covering full lips, was continually pulled back in a smile displaying large white teeth. Unlike Grenville, her legs were crossed, and one kicked up joyfully and periodically, as if to keep pace with a little tune constantly bubbling in her head. "She's great fun," Pop had said, "and good with clients, but not the quality of Grenville."

"I'm going to be very frank with you," I said, shrieking inwardly at this cliché. It had always seemed disingenuous to me, as though the speaker were lying. This was not the case here, and I couldn't let these two women walk out the door without making a valiant effort to stop them. "Pop is seriously ill. He has a brain tumour, and although they can operate, it's done a lot of damage. As he won't be himself, he doesn't want surgery." I paused and looked long and hard at both of them.

Grenville lowered her eyes as if in prayer, and her small mouth became even smaller. She looked as though she disapproved of the entire prospect, which she thought could possibly have been avoided had Pop converted to Catholicism. Ellie Brownwell's bright overbite disappeared, her leg stopped its little jig, and her eyes very briefly misted over. No doubt, I thought, Pop and Ellie had enjoyed some moments together that had prompted Pop's "great fun" comment.

"Pop thought so highly of both of you—your administrative skills, Miss Grenville, and your people skills, Ellie—that I'd hoped you'd both stay on. Pop's neglected things. It wasn't his fault, but it is what it is: a disaster. Is there anything I can do to persuade you to stay? Before you answer, I want you to understand I'll be giving you a raise."

"I've never worked for a woman," murmured Grenville between tense lips, "and you're a very young woman. I'm at retirement age—I'm not sure I can adjust. Your father and I had a good understanding. He was not a hands-on employer, and I appreciated that." The idea of anyone being "hands on" with Grenville was so remote as not to be contemplated.

"Perhaps you should give me a chance, Miss Grenville. Think of it as a final tribute to Pop. If after six months you find me obnoxious, leave, but at least give me a chance. I promise not to be hands-on." I attempted a smile.

"I wasn't implying you'd be obnoxious," snapped Grenville, who was implying exactly that.

"And Ellie? I need your people skills. My husband said I 'don't do nice.' Perhaps you'll be able to help with this. Pop thought so highly of you. If he were himself, he'd really appreciate you staying." Ellie's smile had turned on again.

"We can give it a try for six months. I know what you're like, Dottie. I used to listen to you on the phone when you came here during the summer months. You're not a bit feminine," she gave a slight giggle and the leg jiggling began again, "but I sorta liked it. You've got a 'no shit, Sherlock' approach the clients will either love or hate."

Grenville gave Ellie's bobbing leg a frigid glare.

I looked at them and decided to continue to be completely upfront. "I really need you both. I didn't expect to be thrown into this office on my own without Pop. I have twins, as you know, and I've taken my best friend Angie's son, who's handicapped, to live with us. Angie died in November, remember? My husband's great, but he's a military man and he believes in discipline. Sometimes I feel I'm the house corporal, even private—he was a sergeant, by the way. I'll up your pay by ten percent. The firm can't afford it, but Pop's left a mess and you'll earn it."

"I can wait for six months," said Grenville. "If I decide to stay, it can be retroactive."

"Same for me," said Ellie, but more reluctantly.

"I'm Dottie," I said, "except when you speak to clients, and you're Grenville and Ellie, the same as Pop used to call you, and we're all women together. And if I mess up, I want you to tell me, because I will mess up, you know. You'll stay?"

They nodded solemnly.

What a relief.

Gradually they dribbled in: the house purchasers, some of them happy newlyweds using their wedding money; others who wanted threatening letters written to an intrusive neighbour or an angry jilted boyfriend who wouldn't go away; and still others who were making or changing their wills. "Future estate work," Grenville whispered. "Make yourself executor." And there were also accident victims who had been injured by a drunk driver—a good insurance claim, provided the culprit was insured.

There was no deluge of clients. Pop, I began to realize, had been absent mentally for months and, aside from loaning considerable money—with no security—to losers, had followed up on very little. His practice was relying on hollow promises; his premise of playing it by ear carrying it to a legal abyss.

Ellie had a long list of old clients, and she started phoning them about me. She had another list of clients with outstanding accounts, and she tried to persuade them to pay at least a portion of amounts owing. "Like pulling their teeth out without gas," she complained.

"It's a good lesson for you not to undertake work without retainers," growled Grenville.

The deadbeat recipients of Pop's generosity were never at home. "Taking cruises," sniffed Ellie, who I was growing fonder of by the day, not without feeling a tinge of guilt on behalf of Ma.

Within a month, we hosted a catered afternoon cocktail party for all past, present, and hopefully future clients. It was written up in *The Daily News*, with a special notation that

Dorothy Campbell, formerly Dorothy Butler, Newfoundland's first woman lawyer, would be specializing in family law.

In they came, dozens of them, some who had been waiting for years for an advocate like Dorothy Butler Campbell to protect their interests.

One client was seventy-year-old Peggy Manning. She had left her husband and five children in the jointly owned family home some forty years earlier. The hard-drinking, ill-tempered Vince Manning had broken her nose for the second time when there was no dinner on the table when he arrived home from work. He had remained in their home with a new partner ever since. But the children were long gone.

"They wouldn't forgive me for leaving 'em with him, but I had no place to go. Only two speak to me after all these years. He always told 'em I'd left them, not him, and they believed him—even after seein' all he done to me."

She had a sweet, soft, Irish face and a velour tam covering bleached ringlets, still a pretty woman at seventy. I had thought the stalwart figure sitting next to her with the broad, flushed face and tweed cap was one of the remaining sons, but I was mistaken. It was Cyril, her much younger boyfriend of twenty years.

"You must," I urged, "get your one-half from the house. He can sell it or buy you out. As for the kids, it's strange how a little money starts people talking again." Peggy looked at the smiling Cyril and actually batted her eyelashes.

"We could take that Caribbean cruise we always talked about," she whispered.

Unlike the kids, Cyril had been there.

Unlike Peggy Manning, Theresa O'Reilly refused to leave her six children, aged four to twelve. There would have been more, but she had miscarried twice after two of Tom O'Reilly's drunken rampages. A surly but quiet man when sober, he became a raging maniac after his weekend tavern visits and became aggressive toward her and the ten- and twelve-year-old sons who tried to protect her.

She came to see me on a Monday morning after a particularly rough Saturday night. Her face was covered with bruises, her wrist in a cast. She looked like a war veteran as she limped through the door, a sympathetic Ellie hovering at her side. Her son Dougie, aged twelve, came with her, a cut under his bruised right eye. He looked, I thought with a pang, like Danny Flaherty—a twelve-year-old version—with the same blue eyes, black hair, and crooked smile. "The ol' man," he said cheerfully, "goes cracked when he drinks."

In the waiting room, the other O'Reilly children sat still and wide-eyed. Only the youngest two showed animation as they pulled pages from the various magazines on display.

Theresa was a tiny woman with a shock of dark hair and wild, frightened, blue eyes. Underneath and around the bruises, her skin appeared dead white. She spoke rapidly, driven by nervousness and fear. "He sez he'll kill the lot of us if I sees a lawyer," she whispered.

Her husband had a decent job as a foreman at a local hardwood plant, and they survived on the money he didn't drink away. They even owned their own home, a wooden box surrounded by spruce in the town of Mount Pearl just west of St. John's.

"You've got to get some photos of yourself and Dougie that I can show the judge," I ordered, "and I'll get him out. I'll get you and the kids exclusive possession of the house, and he'll have to pay support for all of you at so much a month. No one should have to put up with this. Good you've got Dougie here trying to protect you."

Dougie rewarded me with a wide crooked smile, and I noticed a missing front tooth. *His father or a fight elsewhere?* "Alex tries too," he said, giving me another smile, "but he's only ten."

"I'm going to prepare some papers for you to sign, and you can go to Tooton's for photos of you and Dougie—we'll cover the cost."

"He'll go off his head when he gets papers," she whispered. "Won't he, Dougie?"

Dougie nodded a solemn "Yup."

"Then call the police," I instructed. I was still young then.

Thomas O'Reilly, defendant in the *O'Reilly v. O'Reilly* motion, which was scheduled to be heard on Friday of that week, was short served with the court papers on Wednesday afternoon before leaving the plant. He discussed the contents of the claim and affidavits with his drinking buddies at the Galway Bay Tavern an hour later.

At ten o'clock that night, the O'Reilly house was a box of flames. He had poured kerosene all around it just to be sure.

Theresa, who slept on the first floor, escaped with the three younger children, but Dougie was burned to death attempting to rescue ten-year-old Alex and his eight-year-old sister, who had been overcome by smoke on the second floor.

The church at Kilbride was packed. Three small caskets lay in front, bearing the charred remains of the three children. I sat with Theresa in the front row, devastated and unable to control my own tears—and guilt.

"I keep thinking I should have called the police as soon as he was served," I sobbed to Wills later. "I asked for a restraining order on Friday's motion, but that was too late. I should have tried to get an *ex parte* restraining order on Wednesday morning, although they hate giving them, especially to me. She told me it wasn't my fault, but that doesn't bring the kids back. And that brave little Dougie..."

Wills stood helplessly in the living room of Angie's Craigmiller Avenue house. Stu and Bobby sat watching me, eyes misty with shared compassion. But Donny snorted, "No way I'd ever be a lawyer. No way."

"Wish you'd give up this family law crap," said Wills,

frustrated and angry. "Even criminal law'd be better. Nothing but grief and aggravation with these families—it's just crazy people doing crazy things. And it's not like you're making money at it."

"What do you want me to do? Defend bastards like Tom O'Reilly? Besides, there's no one else doing it, not the way it should be done."

"There's a reason for that," muttered Wills.

Thomas O'Reilly got twenty years for second-degree murder, pleading alcoholism and temporary insanity brought about by the thought of losing his family as mitigating circumstances. The house, strangely enough, had been insured by Tom in one of his more sober moments. As Theresa had been a co-owner, insurance monies were received. Theresa purchased another home for herself and the three remaining children. We talked when she came in to sign the house papers. "I think of Dougie every day," she sobbed, tears running through the worn fingers of her small hands. "Such a wonnerful boy he was. Father Donahue says he's in heaven for sure, right next to our Lord, wearing a crown for trying to save Alex and Bernadette."

"I'm sure he is," I answered. I also thought of Dougie every day, the wrenching guilt and sadness I felt not tempered by the soothing images of Catholicism.

Both Grenville and Ellie were supportive during the O'Reilly crisis. The Catholic Grenville echoed words similar to those of Father Donahue, and Ellie massaged my shoulders and assured me that, "with a lunatic like O'Reilly," something "awful" would have happened in any event, regardless of my handling of the case. Six months had passed, and there was no talk of a departure or a salary increase.

Harris Snelgrove was my first male matrimonial client. "You'll lose your reputation," giggled Ellie. "You're supposed to be championing all these women. I told Grenville the other day we should have a sign over the boardroom door saying, Women Only."

But Harris Snelgrove was hardly a chauvinistic male, and his wife Sheila was worse than most of the men I fought with. Harris was a clerk with the provincial government branch of the Department of Finance. Before retaining me, he had voluntarily signed an agreement to pay two-thirds of his salary to Sheila and the three children. In addition, they were permitted to stay in the family home until their eight-year-old, Harris Junior, reached the age of sixteen.

Sheila had been given custody, but there were no provisions for child access to Harris. It goes without saying that Sheila's lawyer had drawn up this monstrosity of an agreement that resulted in an impoverished Harris living with his mother and unable to see his children.

"You should have seen me," I scolded. "You should never have signed this without seeing a lawyer."

"Didn't know you took men," he murmured.

"Of course I do," I lied.

I would, I decided, take a select group of men as clients in the future, certainly if they were as docile and put-upon as Harris Snelgrove. In my "women-only" policy, I was as discriminatory as my male colleagues, who I complained about to Wills every night.

Within three months, Sheila had moved another man into the home. Clayton was a big, blustering, hard-drinking longshoreman who, Harris suspected, was "much too rough" on the kids. The agreement had no non-cohabitation clause. The kids had not complained to Harris about their new surrogate father's behaviour as Sheila had not permitted Harris to see them, and threatened him with the loutish Clayton should he venture near the home.

Harris was a pale, slight, nervous man with silver-rimmed glasses and a balding head, and he was always dressed in a dark suit and tie. A typical civil servant, I thought, picturing him behind a desk pouring over figures on the tenth floor of the new Confederation Building. But he loved his kids—there was no doubt about that. During his first visit to my office, he proudly showed me a picture of the family on last year's Christmas card. There were two boys and a girl: the girl a replica of Harris, except for the baldness, and the boys replicas of the large, square-faced Sheila, with her sturdy jaw and broad lipstick-packed smile. She was much too lusty a partner for the pale nervous Harris, I suspected.

"It was sex, or the lack of it," he murmured. "She yelled all the time—morning, night, and all weekend—at me and the kids, so I couldn't perform. It was really embarrassing. Then she said I was a fruit and a faggot, but that wasn't it. It was her and her constant yelling." He blinked rapidly, as if he could hear a chorus of fire engine sirens.

"I will," I assured him, "get you a court order to see the kids every other weekend."

The broke Harris was sleeping in the extra bedroom in his mother's basement. He would have to buy bunk beds for the boys and a proper bed for ten-year-old Evangelina. He would sleep on his mother's sofa upstairs during the children's visits.

Judge Henry, obviously astounded to see me representing a male client, granted the weekend access. He informed Sheila, who appeared unrepresented, that he found her conduct "reprehensible" in light of "the generous support that is being paid voluntarily and your current common-law situation." It was the only time Judge Henry and I had ever agreed.

Sheila left the courtroom in a huff, calling me nasty names under her breath, and I was sure that I heard the word *shark* with a vulgar qualifier. I hoped she knew the meaning of the word *reprehensible* and that she would change her behaviour, but on the next weekend access was refused again.

"They're all sick, that's what she said," complained Harris, his usual pale face flushed with frustration. "It's all lies. They were all at the window crying when I had to leave. Nothing wrong with them that seeing their daddy wouldn't cure."

Furious, I wrote Sheila a letter threatening her with a contempt of court action and possible jail time unless Harris saw the children the following weekend. But on the following Saturday, Harris, who had my home number, as did far too many of my clients, phoned me. He was so upset he could hardly speak. Another one of Stu's hockey games missed, I thought, as I headed for the office.

"Call it all off," he choked. "The kids are all upset, and she says she's going to tell the judge dirty stories."

"Like...?"

"She'll say I tried to have sex with Evangelina and that I'm a child molester. She knows it's not true, but she's probably trying to explain the lack of sex—which she caused. I can't go ahead with it ... trying to see the kids. They'd hear all about it at the office, and I'd have to quit my job. Then everyone will lose." I tried to convince him otherwise, but Harris wiped his pale eyes, now red, and stood firm.

"Some women are worse than some men," I told Wills that night.

"Really," said Wills with an eye roll, "and men pay better."

The Harris story had an interesting, if not happy, ending. A year later, Sheila Snelgrove telephoned the office and wanted me to represent her in having Clayton, the longshoreman, removed from the matrimonial home. "He's beating up on me, a real savage. He even makes Harris look good," she rasped in that harsh gargle she'd used in court.

I told her as Harris's lawyer I had a conflict of interest, and referred her to a new lawyer in town. I knew the source of his fees—child and spousal support. I told her I wanted her to promise me two things. One was that she'd control the yelling, as it put some men off, especially nervous guys like Harris, and two, that she'd take back the nasty lies about Harris and Evangelina.

"Do you think he'd take me back?" she asked, sounding almost eager, certainly incredulous.

"I didn't say that," I answered. "But no more yelling and he just might. He misses the kids. And we never had this conversation."

I ran into a smiling Harris with his kids on Water Street about a year later.

"Things okay?" I asked.

"She really learned something, living with that longshoreman," he whispered. "She's even stopped her yelling. Things aren't great, but as good as I can expect—with her. And I got my kids back."

A happy ending—sort of.

35. Ripples from the Home Front

O VER THE NEXT FEW YEARS, it was said that Dorothy Butler Campbell was "the worst of the new breed of woman" and, even more serious, she was "helping to create discontent within the female population and between the bonds of husband and wife." I had acquired a reputation. I was "aggressive, outspoken, and not respectful" to my learned senior male colleagues. And more seriously, I antagonized the presiding judges, whom I would appeal on principle— and often without money. Angie's trust for women had long evaporated.

"I hope God will reward you, because your clients won't," groused Wills. "Not smart at all—appealing without a retainer. Good thing I'm working for the government."

I knew he was right but I went ahead with my appeals anyway. I knew that even if I won, I'd further alienate the judges, especially Judge Henry, who already detested me. The judges disliked me; they resented seeing a "lady lawyer" in their usual male-only courtrooms. But Judge Henry's dislike superseded that of the others.

He had even confided his dislike to his legal clerk, whose wife was a friend of Ellie's, who promptly passed it on to me. "He says he just hates the sight of you," she chirped, "and you ruin his whole day when you appear before him." Ellie smiled brightly at the prospect. She found working for such a hate-inspiring figure titillating to say the least; it was so much more interesting than working on foreclosures and contracts. Typing my inflammatory affidavits, full of explicit descriptions of drunken abuse and even rape, made her salivate with delight.

"The Great White Shark—that's what the men call you," gushed Ellie.

Grenville sniffed in distaste and disapproval, annoyed by needy women who lacked retainers, and by unprofitable appeals.

I picked up some Chinese food for dinner on the way home. I was late as usual and unable to put up with another of Donny's diatribes about Wills's cooking, which he said resulted in diarrhea—a ridiculous complaint. He was, after all, the only one in the family who suffered from constipation.

"We can't do this every night," complained Wills, addressing the table. "You'd think your mother was getting paid for her appeal work. Nothing wrong with beans and wieners. You know something, guys, your mother and me, we lived on beans and wieners right through law school."

"Another reason not to go to law school," muttered Donny.

"Did you know they call me the Great White Shark?" I said brightly, trying to change the subject while I filled my plate with chicken almond, vegetable fried rice, and garlic and honey ribs, while Donny filled his with double the amount.

"We know," said Stu sadly. "Jerome Tessier yelled it out in the schoolyard yesterday, right in front of everyone. 'Your mother's a great white shark,' he yelled, and Donny had to take him on. He punched him out, right in the kisser, and he had to stay in after school and write lines saying, 'I must not hit my friends.' I would've done it, but Donny's bigger an' hits harder."

"How sweet, Donny," I cooed, "defending me like that," and I deposited some of my spareribs to his plate. "But I don't really mind the shark label—it's really a sort of half-assed compliment."

"Me and Donny mind," said Stu. "This was the second hit for Tessier—the first was when he called Bobby Dumbo."

Bobby looked at us all, waiting for the reaction.

"I'm representing Norma Tessier against Jerome's father," I said to Wills.

"You can't go around assaulting your classmates, son," reprimanded Wills, but he had a slight smile. It was always a mystery to us why Donny was the hitter when Stu was the athlete.

"Defending his mother and brother," I said, giving Donny's thick mop of dark brown hair a little tousle with my free hand, and Bobby's cheek a little rub, as I took my empty plate to the sink. Donny did not reply, but I saw him devour my rib contribution. "Eat up, my luv," I said, and I kissed his warm cheek.

We had grown close since what Wills referred to as our "nutty ghost encounter," even though Donny was the family critic, especially when it came to me.

"Perhaps you should rein in some of your aggression," Wills said later that night. "Can't have your son working toward a criminal record defending you."

"Willy," I replied, exasperated, "you don't understand. It's the 1960s, and they don't want me in the courtroom. It's a male bastion and has been for years—forever, in fact. I'm not that much more aggressive than the guys; it's just how they see me. A man can cross-examine and be as aggressive as he likes and the judge thinks it's just fine. He's seen as very effective. But if I do it as a woman, I'm seen as a total bitch. I'm told to moderate my voice by Judge Henry every time I cross-examine. It distracts and undermines me, but he likes that because he believes I shouldn't be there anyway." Wills shook his head in sympathy.

"The guy shouldn't be there himself. He was appointed

a judge by the Liberals because he was a party hack and bagman—a lousy lawyer, by the way. Perhaps you should think about working for the government. I could get you in." I looked long and hard at Wills. He meant well, but he obviously didn't get it either.

"You've got to be kidding," the Great White Shark replied.

36. The Trials and Tribulations of the Great White Shark

IT WAS WEDNESDAY, the day of the twins' high school graduation. I'd been asked by both boys to confirm my attendance, which meant they believed they'd be getting awards. Donny had already had me check his valedictory speech and Wills had arranged for the afternoon off.

The Heaney trial had been called for the previous Monday. It was not a difficult trial—there were no custody issues, just a sale or exclusive possession of the jointly owned matrimonial home, and child and spousal support. It was scheduled for a one-day hearing or at the most a day and a half. Judge Henry, the only judge available, was presiding.

"Your favourite judge, Dottie," teased Carol, the trial coordinator.

I thought of asking for an adjournment, but Moira Heaney begged me not to. Gerald Heaney had ignored his interim spousal and child support orders, and she was living in a two-bedroom bungalow with her mother and the three children. Her husband, an abusive but well-connected drunk, had full use of the three-bedroom matrimonial home.

Jim Gillingham, representing Gerald Heaney, was a well-known litigator and courtroom nightmare—a motor-mouth who I suspected was being paid handsomely with Moira's missing spousal and child support money. He was, I also suspected, by the exchange of glances and smiles between him and Judge Henry, a personal friend of the judge. As was, it appeared, Gerald Heaney.

"He knows Gerry," whispered Moira Heaney, when she saw the exchange.

"Any preliminary motions or matters?" inquired the judge.

"I would ask Your Honour to confirm he has no personal relationship with Mr. Heaney to dispel any possible perception of bias."

"I find this query both offensive and presumptuous," huffed Judge Henry. "Had that been the case I would have recused myself. We both belong to the Lion's Club, but surely that indicates no perception of bias. What's your position on this query, Mr. Gillingham?"

"The query is offensive in the extreme," sang Gillingham. "I take it that Mrs. Campbell may also object because both of us, Your Honour and myself, belong to the Orange Order and the Liberal Club of Canada."

"I was not involving Mr. Gillingham in my query," I snapped. "I take the answer to mean that you are replying in the negative and have no personal relationship with Mr. Heaney. No offence was intended by my query." I was making a diligent effort to keep the edge from my voice and attempting not to think about the absolute joy of aiming a bullet directly into the ample chest of Judge Henry.

Moira Heaney was nervous in spite of the fact that I'd spent all of Saturday afternoon going over her evidence and financial statement. I had missed another family occasion: Stu's championship softball game.

I presented a financial statement carefully evidenced by slips from Ayre's Supermarket, Gerry having removed all credit cards from Moira's possession.

"Your Honour," crooned Gillingham, "I know I don't need to remind you that Moira Heaney could have obtained these slips from any number of friends. This is hardly valid authentication."

"Moira Heaney will swear these to be her past expenses, and what will be her future expenses if she is living in the matrimonial home," I replied.

"Perhaps we should go forward as if this house is going to be sold, Mrs. Campbell," rumbled Judge Henry, "unless you can show the court evidence of great weight to the contrary. Surely Mr. Heaney has a right to his one-half equity."

"Precisely my position," sang Gillingham.

"I would think, Your Honour, the fact that Mrs. Heaney is unemployed, has never worked, and has never finished high school, is relevant. All the children are with her, with Mr. Heaney's consent, and they are currently sharing one bedroom in the home of Mrs. Heaney's mother. And great importance must be given to the fact that she has received no spousal or child support, contrary to an interim order. Also, I suggest that all these factors should weigh against a sale."

"Mrs. Campbell is giving evidence," crooned Gillingham.

"I suggest," interceded Judge Henry, "that the relevant factor may be violence. I have heard no mention of violence."

"Mrs. Heaney, who will be giving evidence, will inform the court that Mr. Heaney, who has a problem with alcohol, has on two occasions thrown her naked into a snowbank in front of the family home. She was forced to go to a neighbour for help, a very humiliating experience." Judge Henry closed his eyes as if suddenly exposed to a blinding ethereal light.

"And chilly as well," he murmured with a smile. "Do you wish to comment, Mr. Gillingham?"

"Mrs. Campbell is giving evidence again. Of course, we are all used to that by now. I would bring Your Honour's attention to the fact that Mr. Heaney has no criminal record, and has never missed a day of work with the Newfoundland Margarine Company. He's an upstanding citizen, and if anything even remotely out of place has ever occurred, we can attribute it to Mr. Heaney's merely being playful."

I looked at my client, the victim of Gerald Heaney's

playfulness. She looked haggard, as if she had just crawled out from a third snowbank. And it was only noon on Monday, the first day of trial.

"May we, Your Honour, have the morning recess now? Or a brief adjournment? I'm aware it's Your Honour's habit to have a brief morning break."

"Of course, Mrs. Campbell," agreed Judge Henry. It was the first time he had agreed with me in two hours. It was the first time ever, in fact, except for the Harris Snelgrove access issue.

Moira Heaney was a nervous wreck. "That judge hates you," she said in a hoarse whisper, "and he and that bastard lawyer of Gerry's are buddies—I can tell."

"I hate him too," I answered.

"That don't help me," she retorted, quite sensibly.

It went downhill, even from there. The judge accepted all of Gillingham's objections and overruled all of mine. He also permitted Gillingham to cross-examine Moira on her financial statement until she was on the verge of a terminal convulsion.

"My client," I said, "has already answered the same questions time and again. This has reached the point of inflammatory harassment, and I want my objection noted on record for appeal purposes."

I had gained Judge Henry's attention; finally, after six hours, he stopped Gillingham's cross-examination.

On Wednesday morning, Gerald Heaney took the stand, as slick, sober, and well rehearsed as Moira was nervous and hesitant. Gillingham presented him as a paragon of virtue, an excellent father and husband, and a diligent provider for his family. He was a man who never in a million years, would throw his naked wife into a snowbank.

"Liar," croaked Moira in a hoarse whisper.

"Your neighbours," I hissed, "the ones you went to, I'll call them in reply."

"They don't want to get into it, to make enemies."

"Then I'll subpoena them," I said grimly.

"Jesus," murmured Moira.

It was almost noon when I stood up and addressed the court.

"I would ask Your Honour to consider adjourning this case at one o'clock today so I may attend the high school graduation of my sons, scheduled for two o'clock this afternoon. I estimated this trial would be a maximum of a day and a half. I could never have predicted my colleague, Mr. Gillingham, would take so long to cross-examine my client."

"Mr. Gillingham, can you comment on Mrs. Campbell's request?"

"My client," crooned Gillingham, "has taken this week off, without pay I understand, to attend this trial. A high school graduation is hardly equivalent to a university graduation, and certainly not to a law or medical school graduation. I would ask that this trial continue."

"You heard Mr. Gillingham, Mrs. Campbell. I fear I must refuse your request."

"Has anyone ever told you you're a fuckin' arsehole?" I snarled to Gillingham on our way out of the courtroom.

"Many people have," replied Gillingham with a smile, "and if it keeps up I'm going to start to believe it."

"Nice to see you there as usual! I guess you had more important things to do," Donny sneered when I arrived home later. "Better ask Dad or Nan what they thought of my speech—and award. And Stu's award."

I started to explain, but he wouldn't listen. My sarcastic and clever, but hurt, son. I felt so awful and so guilty.

The Heaney case finished on Friday of that week. The Heaney matrimonial home was ordered sold, and minimal child support given. Low and limited spousal support was ordered for Moira, who was given a year to re-establish herself.

"What am I supposed to do?" she wailed.

"Appeal," I answered.

"I got no money."

"I realize that," I replied.

Judge Henry retired after suffering a heart attack the following year. Did I dare hope that in some small way I'd contributed?

37. A Chat with Ma

IT WAS THE AFTERNOON of the twins' university convocation day, which I had barely made, having asked a presiding judge to adjourn my motion so I could attend. His Honour, Judge Martin, had been less than appreciative. It was quite obvious he felt that I would be better off at home doing dishes rather than representing a woman who was fighting her husband for alimony and child support.

Rushing in, I sat down between Ma and Wills in the seat they were holding for me. The ceremony began, starring Donald Alexander Campbell as valedictorian and winner of the silver medal for the most outstanding graduating student.

And now here I was with Ma, missing the graduation formal Wills and I had been asked to chaperone, as it would interfere with my preparation for the following day. I was bone tired and ready to puke with exhaustion.

Ma placed a cup of King Cole tea in front of me, poured in milk, and offered me an arrowroot biscuit.

"Do you ever wonder," Ma asked me softly, "if it was all worth it?"

It was strange that Ma would ask me this, as that very afternoon I had asked myself the same question as I broke the speed limit attempting to reach Convocation Hall on time.

"Yes," I admit, "I often wonder that—all the personal sacrifices and all the guilt. It wasn't just handing the twins over to Angie and then fighting to get Donny's love after her death, it was not doing all those things mothers are supposed to do—things like attending concerts, soccer and hockey games, and school debates. I even missed their high school graduation. The worst was missing Stu score the winning goal for his team at the hockey playoffs."

Wish you could have seen it, Mom, he had said, so sweet and wistful, so unlike Donny. I could have killed myself with guilt and remorse. It hadn't mattered that I had a big meeting with out of province lawyers or that Willy was there. He wanted me.

"A man can miss things because he has a wife who fills up the void," I said. "He's expected to put his work first. A man doesn't have the guilt. It's different when you're the wife and mother. There are things you expect of yourself, and your kids expect, things that you can't do because you're so busy.

"I think about Angie all the time," I continued. "I think about how perhaps I could have protected her if I'd been here and not so absorbed in law work. Perhaps she'd still be alive today—who knows? I can't even think about it, it bothers me so much. And that was before an assault that ended in a hysterectomy. I'll never live that down."

Ma stretched out her hand, a worn hand, her fingers knobbed with arthritis, the product of a thousand immersions in steaming water and Sunlight soap for dozens of years. She rubbed my arm. "It was hard to help Angie when she didn't want to tell you what that awful man was up to. Dottie, you always said you had to help the Angies of this world. Well, I'm sure you have. Gertie Cummings tells me wives threaten their husbands with Dorothy Campbell. I'm sure you've helped a lot of women, women the other lawyers wouldn't bother with. You always said you believed women could be right up there with the men, if they wanted. You said that once, right in front of my church group, remember? And their faces just dropped. I was so proud of you saying that."

"I still believe it, Ma; it's just a matter of time. Remember when Pop was sick? He neglected his clients, so I felt I had to try to keep them, and get some of them back. For two years I worked every night and weekend. Willy cooked dinners. They were horrible, his favourites: canned beans and wieners and fried bologna sandwiches. Donny complained he was vitamin-deprived and probably suffering from scurvy, and even Stu wanted to know when things would be 'back to normal.' Only our sweet Bobby didn't complain. Of course, things never were 'back to normal.' I salvaged the practice—but at a price.

"Women who want a career should have one. And other women should encourage them—just like you and Angie did for me. We can't depend on the men, although Pop was great with me, and Willy's done his best. Angie could have been a professional singer; she had a great voice until she smoked it away. She might have even stopped smoking when she realized it was killing her career.

"Edgar knew exactly what he was doing when he stopped her from teaching her 'sweet little tykes.' She had so little sense of self left that she really only decided to leave him because of Bobby. She let Edgar destroy her, and in the end she hated herself for it."

"So interesting, Dottie," murmured Ma. "I'd never even thought of looking at it that way."

"In fifty years a lot will change. We'll both be dead, but women will be doing amazing things. But I suspect that if they're moms, they'll still have reservations—and guilt—just as I have. There's no such thing as having it all."

Epilogue

I'T's 1973. WE LIVE HIGH on a hill overlooking Topsail Beach, and the wind blows fresh and sharp from the sea: the ceaseless Atlantic, its restless waves seizing the rocks with white furred claws, yet on occasion as smooth as grey silk.

The boys, now large hairy men, come and go. Donny is studying philosophy and wants to be an academic. No fine legal mind here, or if there is, it took a different turn. He is intense and misses nothing. He gives me light kisses when he leaves and on occasion hugs, but only when one of the girls he brings for me to approve is absent.

They look alike, these girls, with mounds of dark hair and porcelain pale faces. They are tiny girls, sweet but not too intellectual. I think of the absent one who died young.

Smiling Stu, his university nickname, promises he'll join me at the firm following law school. He will be well liked when he graduates with his B average. He pats me, makes inquiries as to my stress level, always thanks me for any small chore I perform, and compliments me on my dinners.

He and his father play golf on weekends in the summers. He is Willy's favourite, although Willy denies it when I say so, insisting he has no favourite. His girlfriends are sharp-tongued, intense, demanding. "Not good enough for you," I whisper when they leave.

We still have our little boy, six-foot-two but always six years old. His brothers play ball with him when they visit, and he caddies for Stu and Wills on weekends. He delivers pizza from Pileggi's pizza truck, and delights in the tips he receives, which he shows to us upon his return. His brothers take him to movies and McDonald's. The movies are full of shootings and violence, and they tell me he covers his eyes or ears, depending on the scene. When they are to visit, he gets ready and sits by the door waiting one hour before their scheduled time.

"Is everybody good to you? Who don't you like and why?" Donny always questions him. He is the watcher.

Stu, the kind one, rubs his arm and brings him gifts: miniature cars, his favourites.

Bobby loves Wills. They fish together, and he carries out the gently allocated chores, a willing private to the now-mellow sergeant.

He is my most affectionate child, and we walk together, sometimes near the beach, hand in hand. He once said to me, "I used to think Mommy would come back. But now you're my Mommy, and I don't want you to ever leave."

"I never will," I whispered, looking at his light green eyes in the moonlight and thinking of the emotional connection that we share, of the deep roots of our unconditional love.

And of Angie. He is my gift from her.

Pop drifted away from us, at first forgetful, keeping notations in his black notebook, and then oblivious to life in general.

"Alzheimer's," they said. "It comes out of nowhere."

But they were wrong. By the time they discovered it, the tumour was as big as an orange, but relatively benign.

"If," I asked, "it's removed, will he come back to what he was, funny and smart and playing it by ear?"

They said, "No. Brains don't regenerate. He'll remain the way he is."

We asked him what he wanted, and in a rare moment of lucidity, he said, "No, I've had a good life. Just let me be."

"Don't do it," a nurse whispered. "These doctors, they're too aggressive. He'll be like the rest of them after brain surgery, drooling in his bed."

So we let him be, playing it by ear.

Ma's still with us, living in an apartment attached to our place, visiting for meals. She has aged since Pop's death. There are folds of grief around her mouth and an arthritic "dowager's hump" high between her shoulders that make her look old ... and defeated. But she refuses to move to a seniors' residence. People there may be common, she suspects. Besides, she says that she likes her independence, not considering she has none at all.

I salvaged Butler and Associates, keeping Miss Grenville until a stroke forced her to retire. Ellie still works for me today. I hired two associates, one female—finally, another female graduate from law school who I hoped had read *The Feminine Mystique*.

A wedding and a pregnancy soon followed, and she withdrew.

I thought of Professor Dryden and his comments about women and their personal choices. I hired her husband. He could not withdraw with two dependents.

We do well; we have a good life. Willy's Head Crown. He loves it, although he complains of the weight of his responsibilities and the cavalier attitude of the younger Crowns. He'll have a pension, and he'll retire to the golfing green, with Bobby as caddie.

I hear they call him 'the sergeant' behind his back, hopefully with affection. He never did open his own defence practice.

Hettie and Clement Bennett are both dead. Hettie left most of her monies to Bobby, "in trust," and some to us for "caregiver duties," which was embarrassing as we consider Bobby part of our family, our youngest child. We will take him to Disneyland next year and try to put a dent in all that cash. Later on, we may take him to Europe, Venice perhaps.

He'll like the gondolas and gondoliers and the pigeons at San Marco Square. And I'll like the art galleries.

We have a veranda and on summer nights I stand and watch the water, sometimes like black glass, the moon casting a crystal path across the bay to Bell Island. It's then I see them. They walk close together on this shining path, Danny in his sailor's suit with cap on side, and Angie in her long black gown, arms flaming white in the moonlight. Sometimes they stop and dance, not moving, but swaying together as they did that night so long ago. And then they disappear. But I know they are dancing still, so close, beneath the waves.

We'll meet again
Don't know where, don't know when
But I know we'll meet again
Some sunny day

Acknowledgements

Many thanks to my editors: the superb Bethany Gibson, who supplied her adage of "less is more," much to the improvement of this novel; Colin Thomas, who applied his perceptive insights into characterization; and Laurie Laughlin, who attempted, and sometimes succeeded, in keeping her mother-in-law focused on correct timelines—and on the geography of Europe. And last, but not least, the truly phenomenal Jen Hale, master editor and "fixer," without whose insightful help and dedication this book would never have reached publication. I'll never forget your efforts, Jenny!

I also wish to express my admiration for Renée Knapp, who took over the unenviable job of getting books to publication in the absence of the irreplaceable Luciana Ricciutelli, the editor-in- chief of Inanna Publications for twenty-eight years, and who has shown so much courage and hard work in the process. Also, in memory of Luciana, who went much too soon, and thanking her for her years of dedication to the cause of feminism—and for loving my novel enough to publish it. And thank-you to Morty Mint, my agent, for getting us together.

Lyrics from "We'll Meet Again," songwriters Ross Parker and Hughie Charles, 1939, reprinted with permission of Hal Leonard Publishing.

Suzanne Hillier was born in St John's, Newfoundland, before Confederation with Canada, and before the start of WWII. She attended Prince of Wales College, Memorial University, and then McGill University, where she graduated with a BA in social sciences. This was followed by attendance at Columbia University for postgraduate studies. Following her marriage she lived in Newfoundland and then moved to Toronto where she obtained a teaching certificate, and an MA in English literature from the University of Toronto, all followed by a few years of teaching high school. She entered the faculty of law at the University of Toronto in 1968, one of the few women in a class of 150. She graduated in 1972, the year of her husband's death, and established her own law firm in Brampton, Ontario. She was eventually joined in the practice by her daughter Ava. Suzanne Hillier practiced matrimonial work for over thirty years, and was a well-known trial lawyer credited with many reported Superior Court decisions. In 2005, she retired and started writing, always her primary goal. Her work of nonfiction, *Divorce: A Guided Tour*, was published in 2011, followed by a novel, *Sonja & Carl*, published by Brindle & Glass in 2017. *My Best Friend Was Angela Bennett* is her second novel. She currently resides in Caledon, Ontario. Hillier and Hillier continues to practice in Brampton, staffed by her daughter and grandson, who specialize in personal injury.